DRWG STONES

DRWG STONES

Raven Dane

First published by Telos Publishing
139 Whitstable Road, Canterbury, Kent, CT2 8EQ,
United Kingdom.

www.telos.co.uk

Telos Publishing Ltd values feedback. Please e-mail any
comments you might have about this book to:
feedback@telos.co.uk

ISBN: 978-1-84583-230-8

Dedication

This story is dedicated to Sue Burns, my Cumbrian advisor, Beta reader and owner of the beautiful real Fell Pony mare, Bonbon, aka Waverhead Ebony.

Preface

Our distant ancestors were not fools. Nor did they need intervention from extra-terrestrials to build vast monuments of stone that have defied the ages. These ancient people around the world have left enigmatic reminders of their ingenuity, their courage and their perseverance. The true meaning for their constructions has mostly been lost and open to conjecture, often wildly fantastic, hence the mention of aliens. These monuments were created at a time when humanity had no written records. This was the case for the circle of standing stones in a small field in Cumbria, ones at least had a name. The Drwg Stones, a name passed down from the extinct Brythonic language of the area once known as Rheged.

1

A glass tumbler fell from her hand, shattering into diamond shards and blood red cordial on the flagstone floor. Flora Meade did not notice. Not with a stiletto blade stab to her soul cutting her off from the everyday world, awakening something deep and instinctive within her. She grabbed the side of the sink for support, holding the cold enamel edge tightly, forcing herself to breathe in deeply, to not give into the deep blackout threatening to overcome her.

Stupid bloody fools … she groaned, finally able to steady her shaking hands and recover her senses. There was nothing physical causing this attack of pain and disorientation, Flora was in good health, a fit thirty-two year old. This reaction must be linked to the excavation of nearby Ryecroft field, a warning that someone must have cleaved through virgin soil with a sharp spade. Uncovering what must remain hidden though the reason why long lost to time. The damn fools – curse them all for their wilful ignorance.

Flora cleared up the broken glass and spilt cordial and pulled on a warm jacket. With her two young children at school, there was nothing to stop her going out alone. Though spring's small, wild daffodils swayed among the grass verges, coastal Cumberland had not shaken off the lingering talons of the departing harsh winter. The morning's sunshine had already been interrupted by sharp, sleety showers brought inland from a brisk north easterly wind. As she left her stone cottage home, her constant companion, Bess, a blue merle border collie padded by her side and together they made the short walk away from Eskscale village and up towards the field.

As a child, Flora hated walking past Ryecroft field. The care-free, skipping pace on her way home from roaming, arms full of wild flowers and herbs would quicken to a panic-filled run: never slowing until she reached a wooden post set in the old stone wall that marked its boundary. To an outsider, there was nothing remarkable about the field, scruffy, uneven pasture, overlooked by a now abandoned wartime munitions factory. Yet nothing would have induced her to take one step onto that grass, the earth deep beneath was tainted, uneasy with old, dark secrets that refused to fade over time.

As a young child, she had sensed the wrongness of the place without knowing why. Later, she accepted such feelings as normal. She had learnt from her mother how to understand the old earth magic from the changes of the seasons, the phases of the moon. She also knew what herbs could heal and what could harm. Like her late mother and all her female ancestors. Flora was born to be a wise woman, a witch. Now the adult Flora stood on a roadside grass verge, accompanied by her constant canine shadow. The normally affable and calm collie whined softly, pale blue eyes anxious, her body pressed tightly to Flora's for comfort.

'There now,' Flora soothed the dog with a firm caress as she took in the changes in the field. The green undulations were now churned and chaotic as an army of young lads armed with spades tore into the turf with youthful enthusiasm. Overseeing the dig, Bernard Stanley, their teacher urged them on with enthusiasm bordering on fanatic. The man paced between two groups of school boys, occasionally glancing into a battered note book, and marking out new sites for excavation.

'Areet?' A male voice shouted out a greeting to Flora above the rumble of his tractor as it approached along the road, 'those lads have been busy. Could do with them helping with the potato harvest.'

His arrival did not quell her rising anxiety but she was glad of the company. Jed Barrows, a local farmer, climbed down from the tractor's high seat and joined her vigil at the roadside. 'So the divvys went ahead anyway. They wouldn't be told.'

Flora sighed, her hand reaching down again in an unconscious gesture to caress her fretful dog's head. 'How could they understand, Jed? How can you tell outsiders some things must stay buried?'

'Don't help our case when we can't say why we are flaiten by that paddock,' the farmer replied, scratching the greying dark hair beneath his flat tweed cap.

Like all born in the old Eskscale families, he accepted this field was a bad place. One that had not changed hands over the years but its owner was unknown, maybe an offcomer, an outsider. It was no good for grazing livestock, not one beast of any kind could be persuaded to enter the field. Ridden or driven horses needed to be urged with voice and whip to pass it along the road, shying and spooking with every hoof beat, only calming once clear of the last stone wall.

Most born and bred locals from the old Eskscale families looked to Flora to keep a vigil on the field, to be a guardian on their behalf. He glanced at her, a handsome woman with strong but feminine features framed by Pre-Raphaelite waves of dark red hair. Her eyes were gold-flecked hazel that could soften with compassion or darken and flash with rare anger. She had a timeless quality, an inner beauty and a wisdom that was admired by many. As with so many women, she had been widowed during the last war and left with a son and a daughter to raise alone. Jed had considered courting her, he'd waited patiently, in respect for her loss and now thought it time to make his feelings known. But then came the offcomers. He could see Flora was too distracted and distressed to dwell on romance. Jed had to be content with the friendship that has begun in childhood as both were born and raised in Eskscale.

Catching sight of the silent, disapproving locals, the teacher tucked his notepad into a deep pocket and strode across the field towards them. He lent against the stone wall and beckoned them over but Flora refused to approach any closer. Jed gave her arm a gentle squeeze, 'Shall I send the smug fool on his way?'

Flora shook her head but still held her ground, forcing Stanley to clamber awkwardly over the wall and come to her. Ignoring Jed, his manner was condescending.

'Ah, Mrs Meade, I see you are here to check our wellbeing. Most kind.'

He gave a broad, mocking grin, that Flora wanted to see wiped off his face with a swipe from a well-aimed rancid cod. Stanley swung his arm in an expansive gesture over to the excavation, 'My lads have already found three of the standing Stones. Great work and a tribute to youthful enthusiasm. And strangely none of us have been eaten by primeval monsters.'

Bernard Stanley proceeded to give a mock shudder of

terror.

'Yet. Early days ... things work to their own time out here.'

Stifling a smile at Jed's answering, taciturn remark, Flora strove to keep her temper.

'I see there is nothing I can say to dissuade you, Mr Stanley. I have tried to explain that we are not ignorant, superstitious locals. Indeed, all standing stones should be seen and revered as marvels from our distant ancestors.

She paused for emphasis.

'Just not these ones.'

Stanley laughed, contemptuous of this foolish woman's superstitious nonsense.

'I understand you believe in some ancient boogie men, Mrs Meade ... as you would as the local *witch*,' his emphasis on the last word was an unsubtle jibe, one Flora ignored, she'd been called a lot worse, 'but these stones are part of our national heritage, they will be uncovered.'

Any further conversation was futile, Stanley made a brisk turn away from the two idiotic locals and returned over the wall to his boys. Flora reassured her farmer friend that she was fine and waved as Jed continued his tractor borne journey. She remained by the field for another hour; the sharpness of that first sensation had eased but not her fears. The balance between two worlds that should never meet had been disturbed and the shock waves had only just begun.

Freddie Adams threw his now blunt and mud encrusted spade into the back of the truck. He was too tired to clean the implement first as his teacher always demanded, too desperate to leave this place to care about reprimands and loss of house points. The arduous digging had left the team warm and sweaty, but he felt cold and fearful, a sensation that began from the moment they unearthed the first standing stone.

Groaning, he reluctantly turned away from the school coach waiting to take them back to their school, nestled in a valley at Calderbridge. His mates wanted him to join a group photo around the first stone they had uncovered and restored to its impressive height. He only wanted to get back to the coach with its engine idling, ready to drive away. He never wanted to see the field again.

With the other lads preoccupied with recording their achievement, he turned back to the coach and was within a few yards from safety: his fear stoked by memories of witnessing eerie shadows that needed no sunlight to appear. Of the bone-numbing cold that travelled from the earth through his spade and up into his body when he dug into the ground. Alarm turned to terror as he heard eerie murmuring under his feet, far beneath the soil. Too frightened to call out to his oblivious comrades, too preoccupied with their damn photographs, Freddie picked up speed and hurried toward the coach door.

He took his seat on the coach. The driver, a local man made no query why the boy had left the others. A fleeting look of understanding had passed between them as Freddie came up the steps. At this moment, fear made him almost hate his friends, the fragile relationships he'd made within the old stone walls of Fellview, now an approved school for wayward boys. It seemed Freddie was the only lad on the expedition to experience these strange occurrences. He kept them to himself. His school mates would be merciless to anyone with such fanciful notions, urged on by the spiteful Mr Stanley. His open scorn towards the local people and their warnings about the danger of disturbing the field had permeated the dig. Was he the only one who thought that far from being scare-mongering, medieval turnip eaters, the locals were actually right?

For once, Rowan Meade was not irritated by her younger brother as he dawdled along the village high street on their way home from school. Her mind was too full of anxiety to even notice Ash's seven-year-old antics. She'd hardly taken in the sharp scolding from Mrs Wilson for day-dreaming during her history lesson, normally her favourite subject. Something was upsetting their mother, making her seem so sad, so worried, so distracted.

This morning had been the worse day so far. Her mother had handed over their breakfast in a curious daze, hardly speaking. Her kisses as the children left for school had been loving yet absent-minded. Rowan could see a shadow flicker across her mother's golden-brown eyes, a colour Rowan had inherited. More than that, the acute sensitivity of a wise woman stirred with her soul. She was thirteen, full womanhood was still on the horizon yet she knew what she would become and the prospect both excited and terrified her.

'Tommy said we are all in danger,' her brother broke her musings, punctuating his chatter with kicking a loose cobble stone down the street, adding more scuffs to his leather shoes. As if they could afford new ones. 'Them lads are digging up demons. Horrible monsters that snatch bairdens from their beds and eat them. Raw and still alive.'

'Tommy is an idiot, from a family of idiots.' Rowan sighed, 'All of them tapped in the head and you will be one too if you listen to that nonsense.'

Was it so ridiculous? Hadn't their mother been a central part of the village group who tried to dissuade that offcomer and his pupils from digging up that field and who tried to raise money to buy it off the absentee owner through his or her lawyers? A stubborn person by all accounts who had turned down far more than it was worth. Her thoughts were abruptly interrupted by a more solid disturbance. Stick thin, haggard of face, Mrs Smythe stood in front of the two children.

'Spawn of Satan, it is not too late to repent and beg for God's forgiveness.'

An offcomer married to a local man and now widowed too early. Unlike so many men lost to the war, waggish villagers said Ernie Smythe had been preached to death. Whatever the truth, her lack of understanding of village ways and their respect towards Flora Meade had led to bitterness and a fanatic devotion to her personal version of faith. Loneliness fuelled by her endless indignation appeared to have desiccated her. To the Meade children, she resembled an upright bundle of dried-up flesh and sticks, with the only animation in her glaring grey eyes.

It was sad, Rowan had to remind herself, her mother told her to show compassion to a forlorn woman who needed a cause to give herself a reason to get up in the morning. But why this one? The war was over but its baleful presence had not yet passed. There were grieving families, the hardship of continued rationing. With the munitions factory closed and men returning from the battlefields, the lack of work caused much hardship. There were plenty of good, charitable and local causes for a woman of her energy and passion.

Rowan could see her brother tensing up, getting angry rather than upset despite being a little boy yet old enough to have learned cuss words from the older lads in school. Rowan gently gathered him in a protective embrace and did her best to remember her mother's teaching. Use gentle words against anger …

'Thank you for your concern, Mrs Smythe. It is very kind of you to worry about our souls,' Rowan gave a sweet, guileless smile, 'but we were raised to revere spirits of such love and compassion, there was no need to create a devil to scare us into blind obedience.'

She tried to guide Ash to one side, to step into the road to pass the unpleasant obstacle but the woman was only getting started, 'Ah, but Satan most certainly believes in you and nothing that accursed witch of a mother can say will prevent you both burning in hell for all eternity!'

Rowan tightened her arm around her brother's waist; the old cow was going too far – as always. Mrs Smythe even frequently berated the local vicar, Rev. Winters for not driving the Meades out of the village.

'If your heaven is full of bitter, hate-filled old prunes like you, I'd rather not go. Good day, Mrs Smythe,' Rowan said.

Rowan struggled but managed another sweet smile, hoping her mother wouldn't hear that she had been rude to the woman and pulling Ash with her, headed home. Inevitably, he turned and pulled a face at Mrs Smythe, Rowan did not scold him. Being so young had many advantages.

2

At the Fellview Approved School, Stanley rounded up his digging team, making sure young Adams was included. As usual, the lad became more withdrawn, pale with each mile away from Calderbridge, ignoring the cheery, ribald banter of the other boys. The early morning sky was overcast, with low, brooding, pewter clouds rolling in from the sea. Not a good start, nothing hampered a dig more than heavy rain, turning the freshly turned soil into a slippery quagmire. It would have made common sense to cancel the expedition until later that spring but Stanley was always exasperated at any delay and was impatient to recommence. There was no official deadline but something within him urged haste, an unsettling sensation for a pragmatic man of science. The need for order in his life relied on reason and common sense unlike the superstition ridden villagers led by that infuriating red haired woman.

He had done his best to keep his boys away from the locals but in remote areas like this, rumours seemed to be carried swiftly on the wind. Stanley was eager to continue the excavation as soon as possible. The lads had already dug up the first wonderful find by the stone they had uncovered, a well-preserved Bronze Age axe. Stanley took this to mean the ancestors of these locals had no problem interring their high-status goods among the Stones. If they had not been afraid, why should he?

His move to the Fells had brought a curious fact to his attention. A casual conversation with a local, the caretaker at the school, revealed Stanley may have ancestral roots in the area. Old Jessop had told him that a wealthy branch of Stanley's family were once notable landowners and local gentry not far from this place, even owning Fellview school under another name. Stanley was curious enough to spend time with Eskscale's vicar, researching parish records. None of that wealth was handed down to his own direct forebears, nor did they ever live in Cumberland. Probably just some bizarre twist of coincidence he had ended up teaching at the approved school and not some nonsensical mysterious ancestral connection. He gave an involuntary shudder, became angry with himself for even thinking such a thing, for feeling that brief few seconds of curiosity. Reason and logic had always been central to his character.

For the first time since accepting the post up here in the North West, he missed his old home in East London, even the last school he taught at, situated in a rough, bombed out area of Shoreditch. Tough kids too, born into poverty in the heart of wartime and the horrors of the Blitz, they had endured too much to spare time for fanciful thinking. They had seen enough real terror not to invent any. His time there certainly prepared him to teach these troubled youths at the approved school. A residential institution for young lads who would be sent by a court, usually for committing minor offences but sometimes just because they were deemed to be beyond parental control.

Stanley knew the history of all the boys he taught, of their petty larceny and vandalism, joining violent gangs, being too disruptive for their families to cope with. Freddie Adams was a mystery. Orphaned by the war, like so many other children, he had passed from one family member to another, never staying long before ending up at Fellview. There was no sign of delinquent behaviour, no aggression in the lad at all. He was quiet, studious but with enough about him to stand up to bullying even at the cost of a bloodied nose. His eagerness and interest in ancient history had first made him an enthusiastic volunteer for the Ryecroft dig.

So why the drastic change? From the first day at the site, the boy had become withdrawn, nervous and uncooperative. He preferred to work with his back to the centre of the field, digging by the outer wall for finds rather than help excavate the Stones. Any search for an answer to his odd behaviour was met with a sullen shrug and silence. There was no mistaking a genuine fear emanating from the boy, a fear bad enough to make Adams try to unsuccessfully hide by vomiting in the school latrines before every trip to the dig site. Stanley knew he could excuse him from the excavation but that was not the way to deal with such stubborn insubordination. There was a reason why Freddie Adams had been sent to the school, a reason for his lack of enthusiasm for the dig. Stanley was determined to find out why.

The driver was forced to park the school bus in a tractor passing point along the narrow road by Ryecroft field. This would further annoy the locals but Stanley was not going to risk getting the bus mired in by the mud by parking in the field. As they had approached Eskscale, the first heavy rain drops splattered the windscreen from a dark sky that promised no let up. Having to ask a local farmer's help to tow the bus out of the field with a tractor would be adding insult to injury, this dig was already as popular as cholera among the backward inhabitants of Eskscale.

'Come on lads, we are not going to let a bit of rain stop us, windcheaters on, tarpaulins at the ready. Let's dig up another old stone.'

As the now less than enthusiastic team crossed the wet, windswept field, lugging the equipment they needed, Stanley saw Adams drop back. The boy was shaking with more than cold, his face ashen. Time to stop this nonsense once and for all. He clapped a hand on the lad's shoulder, firm enough to mean business and steered him towards the ring of already uncovered Stones.

'Special assignment for you, young Adams, we have uncovered enough to ascertain where the circle's centre should be. I want you to start a dig there today, see if there is anything of archaeological importance.'

Adams pulled himself away from the master's tight grip. This was insane. Every deep primal instinct within him screamed 'no' … that this was wrongness on a colossal scale. What was the use of warning them? Stanley and his class mates would think he had gone insane. Perhaps he had. Maybe that would be worth it? Taken away in a van by men in white coats to a mental asylum might be the best option. The safest.

'I think that will be dangerous, sir,' Adams stammered, 'somethings are best left untouched. I really think we should leave this alone. I beg you.'

'Idiot boy,' a furious Stanley pushed the lad to one side, 'I have no time for this stupidity. You are just as soft in the head as these inbred locals.'

Grabbing a shovel from the nearest boy, the teacher plunged it into the soil, marked with a flag as the likely centre of the circle. Nausea welled in Adam's gorge, the ground deep beneath him began to pulsate. Overcome he dropped to his knees onto the wet grass. No one else moved, their gaze transfixed on their teacher who was having some sort of fit. Mr Stanley had flung the shovel away and his arms flailed wildly, staggering around on unsteady legs. His eyes bulged, foam bubbling up from his lips from which came nonsensical sounds, almost a language but not one understandable to the horrified school boys. Then he straightened up, retrieved the shovel and restarted digging as if nothing had happened.

No one spoke, embarrassed for their teacher. One of their fellow pupils back at Fellview had severe epilepsy and all had witnessed the boy having a seizure at the school at some point. But never had he sprung to his feet and carried on as if nothing had happened. The lad always needed time to recover in the school's matron's sick bay. One by one, the team returned to the excavation, except Adams, who had run away to be sick behind a hawthorn bush. Stanley left him alone, overcome by a powerful compulsion to remove the soil from the centre of the circle of standing stones. It had to be done, right now with no delay. So obsessed with his excavation, he ignored the team who now stopped what they were doing and watched, mesmerised.

Digging furiously, his shovel hit stone with a resounding clang, loud enough to be heard above the wind and lashing rain. He yelled, demanding a trowel from the nearest lad, and continued his frenzied attack on the soil. There was something there, something large, oval and deliberately buried, even deeper than the Stones. He called for help but the boys held back, alarmed by their teacher's erratic behaviour and agitation. Too overcome with the need to expose the find to the modern world, Stanley carried on without his students help. He sighed in uneasy triumph as he gently scraped away the last remnants of wet soil, uncovering a large burial cairn made from a thick, coarse clay. By trenching underneath it, he discovered the remains of burnt human bones, some flint tools and a broken jet ring. High status grave goods from a long distant past. Somewhere in the background, he heard a boy shouting in alarm but he could not, would not stop disinterring the remains, carefully placing them on the grass beside the cairn stone.

His instinctive warning ignored by his teacher; Adams had backed away as the eerie, pulsing waves of energy coming from the cairn grew stronger with every inch uncovered. It was too much; the strange sensations were increasingly painful to the lad, filling his head with jangling, discordant sounds. So wrong. Those charred bones and objects had been left there for good reason; they should not have been disturbed. The eerie noise and bad energy became unbearable. He fled the field and headed for the village, seeking sanctuary with that woman with the dark red hair, someone he sensed who would not mock his fear.

Whistling to keep up his spirits as he passed the cursed field, Jed Barrows strode through the deepening puddles and cold driving rain. He had travelled most of the way from his hillside farm by pony and trap. As always when visiting Eskscale, he left the faithful Fell pony at a close by friend's smallholding. There was no need to cause distress to the aging but still sound pony by forcing her to pass that accursed Ryecroft field. Now, with Willow settled, tucking into sweet hay in a dry, stone barn, his mind moved onto happy matters. Flora Meade had invited him to afternoon tea at her cottage, a step closer, he hoped, to building their childhood friendship into something more. So much so, that he passed on the opposite side of the road at Ryecroft and focused on the village ahead, lost behind a damp, grey haze of low cloud. A typical Cumberland coastal day.

At the edge of Eskscale, he encountered a bedraggled figure along the road, a young lad, soaked to the skin and doubled over as he fought for breath. Jed recognised the Fellview uniform, now sodden and bedraggled with mud. The boy was ashen, eyes red-rimmed, his thin body shivering with cold and over exertion. He was also clearly terrified. Jed didn't give a damn about authority, never had and he had no intention of dragging the lad back to the dig, surely the cause of the young fellow's distress.

'Reet there, lad, no need to be flaiten. I'll walk with you into the village. I'm sure Mrs Meade can brew up some hot chocolate and find a few cakes to drive away the cold.'

'Is that the beautiful woman with the red hair?'

More than the cold made the boy stutter, his fear was very real.

'The very same. As it happens, I'm on my way there now, so I know there will be hot drinks and cake. But hands off, she's all mine. Or will be, if there is a good god in heaven.'

The lad did not smile or react to Jed's banter, too distressed by what he had fled from. Jed waited until the boy had recovered his breath and walked beside him in an uneasy silence.

Flora had just finished gently lecturing her children to be on their best behaviour when their guest had arrived.

Rowan had already set the kitchen table with their best China and the delicious aroma of baking cakes and scones filled the whole cottage. One of Flora's local ladies had given her two big jars of jam, one greengage, the other strawberry made from last year's harvest, in return for a tincture to soothe her arthritis. Jed's excuse for visiting was also for one of her remedies; Flora had made up a jar of salve to cure his mother's leg ulcers. She was happy to help old Mrs Barrows and to spend time with Jed. She was too young to spurn the prospect of male company, especially such a good man as Jed. Easy on the eye too, with his dark curls, vivid blue eyes, and warm, ready smile.

Bess, the collie, her rival for Jed's affection, whirled around, barking with excitement, announcing his arrival at the end of the front garden. Ash ran to the door to find their guest was not alone. An older boy though not much bigger than him stood slightly behind him, a pale face, wretched looking figure. The unexpected addition made Ash pause, unsure what to do, not helped by the dog's bouncy, rapturous, and noisy welcome. His mother, drying her hands on a linen cloth, eased him to one side.

'Come in, go straight to the fire, you will both catch your deaths in those soaking clothes.'

'I am sure this poor lad could do with the warmth. No need to fuss over me, I'm Eskscale born and bred, Flora, this bit of damp is nothing to a tough farmer.'

He smiled, glad that she saw nothing odd about arriving with one of the lads from the approved school. Little fazed Flora beyond what lay beneath the soil at Ryecroft.

'I wish I had some clothes to fit you,' she dealt with the shivering school boy, 'those clothes need taking off and drying.'

The lad seemed beyond caring, his eyes were wide, body language betraying a deep and abiding fear. And more, Flora was aware he was a natural sensitive, gifted … or cursed with the Sight. He would have seen spirits since early childhood and known by now they could do no harm. Something else had triggered this trauma. She pulled up two wooden stools and bade him join her by the fire. It had to be connected to the standing stones.

'Ash, Rowan … look after our other guest, please, the tea is ready to pour and the cakes cool enough to eat. Just save some for me and …?'

'Freddie … Freddie Adams. I shouldn't be here …'

'Well, you are here now, Freddie. Time enough for afternoon tea and to get nicely warmed up.'

Flora waited until the lad was warm before taking him to one side, out of earshot of the others. He had stopped shivering but his face remained pale, his dark eyes wide with fear. She stayed silent but reached out and held one of his hands, letting him feel her strength and honesty, something a lad this sensitive would understand instinctively. He carried a burden; one he should not have to endure alone. Hesitant at first, Freddie blurted out all he had experienced on all the Ryecroft digs. That morning had been the most dramatic. He carefully told Flora about his teacher's fit and mania afterwards. Freddie also tried to describe the powerful, hostile sensations that had assaulted him from the desecrated cairn. A curious calm descended on the boy, his voice grew quiet, strangely older and distant, as if channelling another's thoughts. His London accent softened to another, one closer to that of the indigenous farming families.

'So much emotion, wave after wave of despair. Our

ancient ancestors had made an extreme sacrifice, one that broke their hearts to seal the centre of the Stones. Their spirits howl now at what terrible damage the *Saesneg* have done, they cry out in anger, sorrow and in warning.'

His voice trailed off and his composure returned to that of a frightened lad. Flora decided not to question him, she doubted if Freddie would even remember what he had just said. How would he have known the old Cumbric word for the Anglo Saxons, the English? Someone had reached out from the distant past and used him to send out a warning. Rowan called out from the kitchen that the tea was ready, a timely interruption. What the lad needed now was something normal to reground him to the present.

After the welcome hot tea and food, Jed had taken him back to the dig on the boy's insistence, where his absence appeared not to have been noticed. The farmer watched as Freddie joined the rest of the bedraggled team packing up their tools, then rocking the bus to get it moving away from the sodden ground. Even the layby where it had been parked had become waterlogged. He considered offering his own strength to the effort but an unsettling, hostile glare from their teacher made him back off. There was something odd and unnatural about the gleam in Stanley's eyes. Something significant had happened today and it would not be good.

3

As if the outrage of harbouring a self-proclaimed witch in their small community was not bad enough, now the village was further damned by the heathen circle of ten stones. Brazen, ugly things some good Christian in the past had wisely buried. Mrs Smythe had waited until twilight before venturing along the farm track towards what was now called Ryecroft Stone Circle. She was alone, the families who lived in a nearby row of tied farm cottages would be asleep, the men too deep in their cups by now to notice the quiet tread of a woman in the dark.

As she made slow progress, her mind still seething. Those officials who supported the dig insisted the stones must be uncovered, had told the hostile villagers the things would bring in tourists, prosperity. Villagers that mumbled superstitious nonsense about old curses. One even mentioned a buried pagan god. All that idiocy would stop tonight. Geraldine Smythe would see to that.

The dark held no fears for her, not with sweet Jesus guiding her way, holding up the lamp of righteousness. In her hand was a large tin of red paint. Her plan was to ruin the Stones for the prospective tourists and calm the fears of the locals. There was nothing here a strident red cross on each stone would not stop. Symbolically of course. The devil existed but not the pagan deity whispered about in secretive local legends.

Without giving away her plan, she had tried to enlist the help of the local vicar but that fool Winters would have none of it. He'd found a way of keeping his small and scattered flock by not dismissing their ridiculous fears. The man had no backbone, no strength of faith.

By the time she reached the stone wall around the field, full darkness had fallen. She checked her battery-powered torch and after a good shake, it flickered into life. The weakness of the beam now out in the country disappointed her, it had seemed more than up to the job in her kitchen earlier. Mrs Smythe considered returning home, the Stones could remain untouched one more night and day while she found a better, more powerful torch in the village shop.

She chided herself for her weakness and lack of resolution, it was not that dark. After the days earlier heavy rain, the skies had cleared during the early evening. The fresh smell of washed vegetation felt like a rebirth, a baptism, all good omens. Even better, there was a full moon rising on the horizon whose light that would aid her plans. With surprising agility, she clambered over the rusty five-barred metal gate into the field and strode across the sodden, slippery, uneven grass to the nearest offending standing stone. That she did not trip over the unruly tangles of nettles and solid clumps of burdock or stub her toes on the churned-up earth was another sign of the righteousness of her mission.

Reaching the first stone, she placed the heavy paint tin on the grass, rested her hand against the coarse surface as she caught her breath. There were no strange vibrations, no portent of danger. As she knew all along, it was nothing but a chunk of rough-hewn grey Borrowdale rock. She pulled out the paint brush from her coat pocket and tried to prise the tin open with her fingernails, splintering two in the process. Forbidden to curse by her faith, Mrs Smythe discovered a flaw in her plan. She had forgotten how tightly new tins of paint were sealed.

Before she could come up with a solution, a shadow flickered at the edge of her vision. Startled, she turned but there was nothing but the night. Scolding herself again, she rifled through her handbag, relying on touch to find anything she could utilise to get that tin open, a metal comb, a nail file. Again, a shadow glanced past her, this time in front of her ... silent and without form, as if part of the night had merged into a separate entity. An owl, hunting on silent wings, Mrs Smythe rationalised, but it was enough to put her nerves on edge.

She decided to go back to the village, return on another night when better equipped and the moon was full enough to light her way. She bent down to retrieve the paint tin ...

Pockets stuffed full with pebbles; two lads sauntered along the lane leading to the now abandoned munitions factory. The last lorry from the War Office had left during the week, with every piece of equipment worth salvaging finally removed. More importantly for the boys, the army personnel guarding the place were gone, re-assigned to more important post-war duties.

It was spring, the days were getting longer and the twins looked forward to the weekends for their mischief making. Today was a school day but they had bunked off, knowing their ma would make an excuse for them. Stevie and Clive Thwaite were ten, both were rumoured to have inherited their tousled, thick mops of bright orange curls from their real father, a local farmer. The unproven wanton Mrs Thwaite was married to a local man with resolutely dark, straight hair. Their younger brother, Bert, looked the spitting image of Ed Thwaite. There were some at school who once tried to tease the twins, call them the Carrot Tops, or far worse, a big mistake, their lesson hard learnt by receiving black eyes and split lips.

The boys had grown up tough little bruisers, relying on nobody but each other. Always in trouble, their escapades were always part of local gossip, the Thwaite twins were wild as cats and with no respect for their elders and betters.

'Do you think them monsters from the Stones are real,' ventured Stevie for the umpteenth time that morning, his fascination for the macabre stronger than his brothers.

'Nowt there that can't be seen off with a well-aimed stone,' replied Clive, unbothered that he had already said that many times, they never argued, not with the world as their enemy. 'Now shut yer mouth and keep an eye out, we don't want some gammerstang ruining our morning.'

'Did you remember to bring the scran?' demanded Stevie, pinching his twin's arm. Clive pushed him away roughly then patted a square bulge in his coat pocket, 'Ma's made us sandwiches and I nicked some apples from Old Mrs Lassiter's shop window.'

Stevie held up his own stolen treasure, also from the same shop run by an elderly lady high on trust and low on eyesight and hearing. A large bottle of fizzy pop, Tizer by its luminous orange hue. The opaque, thick glass bottle would become ammunition once empty, no point trying to return it to the village's only grocery shop to claim a penny back on obviously stolen goods. Mrs

Lassiter still had a sharp memory for financial transactions.

The boys continued their mission, strolling along the quiet lane, kicking stones and hitting things with sticks. The wind had changed direction during the night and they soon felt the first true warmth of spring through their layers of clothes. Reaching the abandoned munitions factory, the twins sat on a wall, removing their jacket, soon followed by their well-darned jumpers and drinking deep of their purloined Tizer. Clive's attention wandered from the austere sides of the works and their tempting yet unbroken windows, to the field a hundred yards below. To the uncovered Stones.

He shivered despite the sunshine, triggering mocking laughter and a punch from his brother, 'daft apeth! You don't believe in all that demon talk … or do you? You big babby!'

Stung by Stevie's jibes, the lad leapt down from the wall, folding his arms. 'Babby, am I? Well, let me see you walk down into that field, right up to the nearest stone … give it a reet aald kick.'

'Ok … I will.'

Stevie's reply was hesitant, bravado draining by the second. 'But only if you go too.'

His brother's challenge had backfired spectacularly. Clive could not refuse without looking a babby, a coward. He swallowed hard, mind racing. It was still only an old field, even with those large stubby stones sticking out of the still churned up ground, like dinosaur teeth. No one had actually seen anything bad; it was all just grownup talk in overheard whispers. And grownups could be really stupid. Like when the local idiot Jarvis Brookes thought the Nazis had landed on the beach and made Rev Winters ring the church bells to announce an invasion. Since when did Nazis look like grey seals?

Clive answered the challenge by vaulting over the stone wall into the field, walking confidently towards the Stones. To his satisfaction, his twin had hesitated and was still on the other side, standing in the lane with his mouth wide open. Who was the babby now? He bellowed in triumph, 'Who is the flaiten little bairden, eh?'

With a more confident spring in his step, Clive sauntered to the nearest standing stone and taking a stone and catapult from his pocket, hit it squarely in the centre. He flinched at the slight pinging sound of a ricochet but relaxed when nothing monstrous emerged from the ground to chase him. Emboldened he strode closer to the stone and gave it a hearty kick, his bravado earning him little more than a stubbed toe. By now Stevie had wandered over, his face pale beneath his ginger freckles. It was broad daylight, he'd reasoned, bad things like monsters and demons did not attack little lads on sunny mornings ... did they?

With his new confidence, Clive began to explore the field, maybe the school lads had dropped things from their pockets while digging out the Stones, a few pennies or a penknife would be treasure for the twins. Stevie followed with less enthusiasm, reluctant to push his luck. Something caught his attention in the centre of the stone circle. He grabbed Clive by the arm and pulled him towards the indistinct shape in the long grass.

Flora returned to the village, both of her children in tow after taking some medicinal cordial to an elderly widow with bad rheumatism who lived on a nearby farm. In return, Rowan carried a small rush basket of freshly laid brown eggs and Ash had picked up some iridescent blue green rooster feathers to make into a headdress for the school pageant. Their happy mood evaporated at the sight of the village in turmoil, with seemingly every inhabitant out on the main street, surrounding a harassed Sergeant Brodie, the local beat bobbie. The sight of so many police cars and motorbikes from nearby Whitehaven added to her anxiety.

Sending the children back to their house, Flora walked into the centre of the commotion, sensing fear and anger from the villagers. Jenny Huddleston, the infant's teacher took her to one side. 'Terrible, just the most terrible thing that has ever happened around here ...'

Jenny broke away, tearful and clearly unnerved. The older woman gave her a light hug and went to seek more information from someone with a cooler head. Could her nightmares about Ryecroft be turning to a chilling reality so soon? She caught a glimpse of the ever-reliable Jed Barrows and took him to one side.

'Nasty business,' he sighed, shaking his head, 'the police are trying to cover up the worse of it but word has already got out and spread from them red headed tearaways who found her. What was left of her, that it.'

Flora curbed her impatience, taking your time was a local trait, some things could never be hurried, especially good gossip or tragic news.

'Her head was pulled clean off, they said, her neck stretched and twisted like a corkscrew ... what could do that to a defenceless woman, Flora?'

He continued, 'the Thwaite twins found her lying in what they said was a pool of blood, quite a shock to those little tykes. Might keep 'em quiet for a while though.'

Flora took his hand, gave it a gentle squeeze. 'Who was it Jed? Who did the lads find?'

'The Bible thumper, that poor, sad widow, Geraldine Smythe,' he replied, 'Police found her head a full twenty foot away from the body. Nasty business indeed.'

He bent down to whisper something the police authorities now in charge of the case did not want as common knowledge.

'The body was surrounded by a pool of red liquid, but it were red paint, spilled from a can she had been holding. First medic on the scene said there was no blood left in her at all.'

Staggering back, her mind reeling with the horrific details of the poor woman's death, Flora fought back the taste of rising vomit. No wonder young Freddie Adams had been so frightened. Evil had risen with the Stones and it had claimed its first life. Would that be enough to appease it? Or would it demand more? Whatever the truth, this was a time to stay calm and focused. This was a small community, close knit to the point of claustrophobic. Unity and a sense of purpose, of doing something had to prevail.

Flora sought out Rev. Winters and Sergeant Brodie to join her and Jed for an initial emergency meeting. It was time for all those of the old Eskscale blood to gather to pool their knowledge and prepare to fight back. Some deep instinct warned Flora this gruesome death may not be the only one, innocent lives lost to whatever haunted those uncovered Stones. They met at Jed's farm, gathering in the kitchen, warm from a large, lit range around which three pet cats and the huddle of farm dogs slumbered together in cosy contentment. Jed brewed up a pot of strong tea as the others settled around a wooden table. Flora sensed some embarrassment in her friend's eyes. He lived alone with no housekeeper to help with domestic tasks while he worked long, hard hours out on the Fells. The house was clean enough but untidy and the kitchen reeked of wet dog. Jed had no reason to be uncomfortable around her. She understood.

Once settled, the grim mood deepened more as Sergeant Brodie spoke first, his big hands cradling his stoneware mug as if gathering comfort from the warmth.

'The other old Eskscale families are closing ranks. Stubborn as overworked mules. They reckon once the history lads have left, everything will settle down and be as before.'

'They may well be right,' agreed Flora, 'but would it not be wise to be prepared if something seeks more innocents to kill? Something or someone drawn by the evil awakening beneath the earth.'

'But how do we stop it?'

Jed's remark hung above them like some mythical sword of fate. He spoke again.

'And more importantly, can it be stopped?'

Grabbing a local newspaper from a startled boy in the front row, Stanley scrunched it up into a ball and stuffed it in a wastepaper bin.

'Stuff and utter nonsense!'

Freddie paled as his teacher addressed the class. The man's attitude was not unexpected but unwelcomed by the young lad. Even this horrible news would not put Stanley off excavating all the Stones and then look for any more artefacts buried in the soil: a normal dig anywhere else but Eskscale, one Freddie would have enjoyed.

'A very nasty incident by all accounts,' he continued but no reason for our important work to be held up any more than it has already.'

The discovery of a bloodless, decapitated, mutilated woman's body among the excavation was a sensation, one that had distracted the other pupils into excited speculation over the possible culprit. Not so Freddie. This was not the work of a deranged maniac, a rabid wild animal, or a frenzied robbery gone wrong. This was supernatural forces at work. The lad never felt so alone. Fitting in with the other boys at school was a vital survival tactic. A quiet, small fourteen-year-old, with poor eyesight hid behind ugly spectacles with thick glass lenses, a conscientious student with a stutter at times of stress. One who could sense the presence of earth-bound spirits wandering the corridors and dormitories of the old building. Harmless shades of past inhabitants unable or unwilling to pass on from this earthly plain. Such a boy would be an easy target for bullies among both his classmates and teachers.

So, he had always done his best to pitch in, enduring the rough and tumble of the football pitch, the cuts and bruises, the mud and freezing cold after match showers without complaint. He marched with the school's army cadets, refusing to wince at his blistered feet pinched by hard, ill-fitting leather boots. He joined in the back breaking archaeological dig at Ryecroft field out of both duty and his own curiosity. The past fascinated him, especially as he was surrounded by the fading shades of the bygone inhabitants of the hall. They did not frighten him; they were just sad and inoffensive. What haunted the Ryecroft Stone circle was far from harmless. Something freed from imprisonment beneath the soil, it had shed its first blood for hundreds of years. Would that be enough? Somehow Freddie doubted it

Frustrated by the delay caused by the murder incident with the field cordoned off as a crime scene by the police, Stanley paced the empty staff room. A much-needed cup of tea sat forgotten, stone cold on a table. That idiot boy showing off to the others with a purloined local paper had annoyed him, feeding the ridiculous atmosphere of superstition and fear that surrounded Ryecroft Stones. At first, he had felt nothing wrong about the site itself, a sodden field, constantly salt wind - blown and wet from the Irish Sea. His new obsession for uncovering the Stones was a different matter, something deep and important in a way these foolish yokels could never understand. Indeed, neither could he. Since uncovering the charred bones beneath the central stone, his mission to restore the Drwg Stones occupied his every waking thought, his nightmarish dreams when the dark thoughts allowed him to sleep. And what dreams. Blurred, chaotic images of spilt red blood and faceless shadowy creatures with raking talons. Of a thunderous voice echoing through his body that demanded to be obeyed. The language was unknown to him, yet somehow its commands were branded on his soul and became an intricate part of him. So deeply and indelibly imprinted, Stanley no longer had the ability to defy them. His free will had been obliterated. He had no choice but to comply.

4

Summer 1949

Jed Burrows sighed as he picked up a handful of warm, dry soil. It was only July but the long, hot summer days had already reduced his grazing land to an arid, yellow sward when it should have been lush and green. There had not been enough fresh, new grass ready to get the first cut of hay for the winter … always on a livestock farmer's horizon in what should have been a time of plenty. The sky was a cloudless blue, a background for whirling, darting swifts, no shortage of insects for those graceful visitors.

As he glanced around at the land below his pasture, from his high vantage point, he could see a cavalcade of dumper lorries leave the munitions factory laden with broken slabs of concrete and bricks. The site was being demolished, though for what reason was unknown, even to the most successful gatherers of gossip in Eskscale. Was it to reclaim the land back to agriculture or had the government made new plans for the site? Jed hoped the latter was true; post war times in rural Cumberland had few opportunities for working age men. He looked back at his flock. A quality herd of tough Herdwick sheep, native to the Cumberland Fells. This year's lambs were still on their mothers. He whispered a prayer for rain to any deity listening; the lambs would need grass when it became time for weaning as would the ewes already pregnant with next spring's arrivals.

Jed could not help looking down at the newly unearthed stone circle on Ryecroft field in front of the munition factory site, they had the power to draw the eye to them, regardless whether you wanted to or not. They made him shudder. To a new visitor, they would appear to be harmless slabs of stone. That impression never lasted long, the closer they got to them, the more the unsettling was the atmosphere emanating from them. Thankfully this seemed enough to prevent most outsiders from wandering into the field, ignoring the 'Keep Out, Private Land' signs. In Eskscale itself, talk of new strange goings on had ceased but he knew Flora's vigilance had not lessened. As their fledgling romance grew, so had Jed's understanding of what she endured every waking moment and haunting her dreams. This was an uneasy false calm, what would follow still an unknown.

He felt a gentle nudge against his hand, Moss, his black and white border collie was politely seeking his attention. He followed his brown eyed gaze to see a welcome figure with her own collie, Bess, approaching him. Flora, unmistakable with the burnished copper of her hair glinting in the sun. His heart thumped so hard she should surely hear it as he strode down to meet her. She was a wise woman: she must have sensed his great love for her though no words had expressed it. As he neared, Flora held up a wicker basket and spoke with mock seriousness.

'I'll not have you gasp your last up here from thirst and heat stroke, Mr Barrows.'

Jed smiled and joined her sitting down on the warm, dry ground. The two dogs, already close canine friends settled close by after canine sniffs of greeting. Pulling aside a red and white gingham cover, Flora brought out a brown and cream stoneware jug.

'My own fresh strawberry cordial, as cold as I could get it in this weather. Also, I have some bread I baked this morning and smoked cheese from Old Ainsley's dairy and your favourite, a whirl of Cumberland sausage.'

The farmer started to protest at her kindness out of politeness but Flora uncorked the jug and handed it over.

'Take a good long swig while it is still cool. And I am not lugging all this food back down the fell. We share it all now or I'll leave it out for the wildlife.'

'Ay, there's many a beast or fowl would appreciate summat to eat.' He looked across to Bess and Moss, "But I suspect our collies will finish it all.'

He kicked at the dry soil with the heel of a stout boot.

'We'll all be in trouble if it doesn't rain soon. Reckon I'll not be keeping any of this year's lambs and none left to grow on till autumn.'

Flora did not reply, understanding Jed's unease. He'd yearned to build up the size of his flock now war was over. Feeding the hungry, besieged British public had been a priority, increasing the ewe herd by keeping female lambs to grow on and stay with him had been a luxury he was unable to do. She looked up at the aerial dance of the swifts, beautiful and seemingly joyful as they rode the thermals. The warmth of the sun on her face and of the earth beneath her felt so good, too good to be mournful. Jess stood up between them, hackles up, a low wuffle in her throat.

'Just a grass snek, Jess, let it be,' Jed murmured, 'summer is the snek's time to thrive. It won't harm us or the sheep.'

Flora smiled, that was so like Jed. No thought of

killing the large snake as so many would do. He was right, it meant no harm and was revelling in the long, hot days.

'Of you go, *Nedir*, enjoy the sun while it lasts.'

That was like Jed too, a son of countless generations of Cumbrians, way back to the time it was a Brythonic country, speaking a language close to Old Welsh and Cornish. His ancestors' word for snake had survived now as a local nickname for the reptiles. Her thoughts returned to the less welcome aspect of the long hot days and nights. Many locals had come to her door recently, farmers and growers wanting her to work a miracle and cast spells to bring on rain. This she could not and would not do even if she had the power. Only the Mother could control the ebb and flow of the natural world, snakes and lizards had their rightful time in the sun as did the insects on which so many creatures needed to live and feed their young. Only the Goddess could bring balance: Her ways not to be questioned by the arrogance of mankind.

She pushed aside such thoughts as they ate their lunch in a relaxed, comfortable silence, too much at ease in each other's company to need to fill the air with small talk and gossip. Flora laughed as she lay back on the warm earth, her hair spread out behind her like a burnished copper nimbus.

'I carried that food up the fell just for you, and look what a piglet I am. I've eaten most of it.'

'There was more than enough for two.'

He replied with a grin. Flora reached across and held his hand, one roughened by years of hard work and harsh weather.

'And when exactly are you going to kiss me?'

Jed's dark eyes widened at such a direct approach. He

thought he had been careful to shield his feelings towards Flora. She was a war widow; her grief was to be respected. Not all women in her position wanted a new relationship, concentrating on raising their children alone. But she had broken through that barrier of deference with a question spoken not in jest, she meant it, welcoming him with the gleam in her amber eyes and hesitant, questing smile. He murmured his answer ...

'How about now?'

The hot summer brought a record number of tourists to the Lake District. So many that those seeking a more off the beaten track experience left the popular Lakes and followed the ancient Fell tracks down towards the sea. They would find beautiful, wild vistas along the rugged coastline at St Bees. To the dismay of Eskscale residents, many wandered into the village, following carefully scrutinised unfolded maps, looking for places of interest. If it wasn't for the wretched Drwg Stones, these tourists would have been most welcome. The seaside village could grow, reopen the hotels and guest houses, restaurants and other attractions bringing most welcome employment.

Uncovering the Stones had released a blood drenched curse that all the old families now accepted as real and inevitable and some of the newer ones had even begun to believe in. How could they not? Even if the only life lost since their exposure had been the gruesome murder of Mrs Smythe the very air above Ryecroft Field felt toxic, tainted and dangerous. Some people sensed a new vibration of the earth within the stone walls that enclosed it, a pulsation that leached out beyond its confines. That would explain the agitation animals felt when in proximity of the field and why no wildlife lived there … not even rabbits or resilient rodents. No birds would alight there or even fly over it. Even its few, tough wildflowers had wilted and died with no insects willing to seek pollen in the field. Only yellowing rough grass clung on to cover the soil and many expected that to die off completely even if it rained enough to revive the plant life in surrounding fields.

Henry Eldred, sturdy wooden staff in hand, strode along a route across the Fells made from centuries of movement, flocks of sheep, pack ponies and the footsteps of countless humans. This was the way he loved to travel, along a well beaten but empty track with only swallows, ravens and raptors above him and the scurry of startled rabbits beside the path. He had been a regular visitor to this wild, remote land before the war when he could trek all day and not meet a soul. Now on his return, he was recovering mentally and physically from serious wounds received driving the Nazis out of occupied North Africa. To his dismay, Eldred discovered the Lake District had been transformed. The narrow roads to the picturesque villages of Grasmere, Ambleside and Keswick were choked up with coaches packed with tourists. The serenity of iridescent Lake Windermere now shattered with the smoky chuff of steam powered pleasure boats. Its banks crowded with every Tom, Dick and Harry along with their wives, broods of boisterous children and barking dogs. Once pristine grass had become a depositary for abandoned rubbish and dog excreta. Good for the local economy, Eldred conceded but not for a man who needed the peace of a true wilderness to mend his damaged soul.

He could feel his spirits lift with every step away from the crowds. He revelled in the drone of bees on bright yellow gorse with its intoxicating coconut scent. Above, he heard the piercing cries of a pair of peregrine falcons in their graceful aerial dance, riding on thermal uplifts. He walked with a noticeable limp from a land mine shattered leg but his joy at being alive and free overrode the pain. No medical therapy could compare to this wild splendour.

Eldred walked all day, pausing only to drink crystal clear water from tumbling becks and eat some of the precious, energy restoring Kendal mint cake he was able to obtain in the brief few months of sweets being available without rationing coupons that April. As the day progressed and shadows lengthened, his mind turned to seeking a place to spend the night. He had not brought camping gear, too burdensome to lug on his long treks. He planned his walk to take him off the wild Fells and head down towards the sea where fishing villages and small towns could have guest houses or inns ideal for a lone hiker. Pausing to unfold a map, he noticed this path would take him close to a village called Eskscale, why did that sound so familiar? He thought back and remembered the excitement reported only in the better newspapers, of an unknown circle of Standing Stones uncovered by a local team of schoolboys. That confirmed Eskscale as his destination, something new to see and record in his notebook along with his sketches of dramatic Fell mountains and magical waterfalls in wooded glades. In his opinion, there was nothing on his tour of war torn, fly blown North Africa that could compare to the serene beauty of the British Isles. By choice, there were no friends or family that would contradict him. He still had horrific nightmares that made him bellow out aloud in torment, why inflict that on a wife and children?

By the time he had reached the outskirts of the village, he was more than ready to relax at a pleasant hostelry, maybe a long soak in a hot bath if they had one. He passed a few large Victorian buildings along the sea front that looked like they may once had been hotels but were now boarded up. Casualties of the war maybe. Eldred found a central square which had some sign of life, two pubs and what appeared to be an up and running guest house. The aromas of beer and cooking food was another hopeful sign. He walked across the cobbled street to the nearest pub, a solid, old, grey granite building with a well painted hanging sign of a curly horned, white-faced sheep. Not surprisingly it was called The Herdwick Tup after an old local ovine breed. He walked into the bar area which had remained unchanged for decades with its stone walls, polished beams and bar adorned with gleaming brass fixtures. A warm welcome too, from both the friendly landlady and the customers, a pleasant change from some less hospitable local pubs in other rural settings. None of the dreadful silence a stranger sometimes endured when arriving, the air taut with hostility to any outsiders.

He ordered a pint of whatever was local to the area.

'That will be a pint of the best the Jennings Brothers can brew,' answered the landlady, introducing herself as Maggie Graham. 'Been here in Cumbria since 1828, so they must be doing summat right.'

Eldred took a swig of the beer and smiling, nodded in agreement. After his long hike it tasted heavenly.

'I bet you could do with some supper now. I have a home baked shepherd's pie in the oven ready to serve, nothing fancy though.'

'That sounds wonderful, Mrs Graham and worth the long walk just to taste it.'

He took his pint to an empty table and felt every ache in his damaged leg and back muscles begin to make themselves known. Eldred did not mind the pain, it showed the damage from the bomb was healing, torn ligaments and muscles knitting back together. His mental state too was recovering, at no point on his long ramble across the Fells did his mind flash back to dreadful wartime memories. He could not remember feeling this good for a very long time. Perhaps he could relocate to Cumbria, there was nothing holding him in Basildon. Mrs Graham came over, carrying a steaming, aromatic platter of potato and lamb pie. After thanking her, Eldred asked about accommodation in the village. The smile left the landlady's broad, honest face.

'Oh sir, I am so sorry. There hasn't been much call for visitors since the war. But we had four rooms above the bar and six at Annie and Trevor's guest house until yesterday. They were all booked by the Government, a load of men in suits have arrived to survey what was the munitions factory. Won't say why though, very hush, hush.'

She sighed, 'But we are used to that around here, what with the factory being so vital to the war effort. As long as they bring jobs for the locals, we will be content enough.'

Mrs Graham shook her head.

'That don't help you sir, does it.'

'You've missed the last train to Whitehaven, sir,' she continued, 'but I am sure one of the lads would be happy to drive you there. Won't you my fine *marras*!'

A few of the locals raised their pint glasses and tankards in cheerful assent. Eldred had already known that 'marra' … was a local term for friend. Eldred clocked up their readily offered hospitality as another good sign that he should move here. However, Whitehaven, an attractive but busy coastal town was exactly what he was trying to avoid. It would be packed full with tourists now.

'There is no need to bother anyone, Mrs Graham, it is a fine night for camping.'

It was a warm summer night with not a cloud in sight, it would not be the first time Eldred slept under the stars.

On hearing this, the woman's ruddy features appeared to blanch, her hands tightened into fists from tension, not anger.

'Of course sir, as you wish. As you say, it is a warm, dry night. You will get a view of the stars like no other with our clear, clean air. I'll make you a flask of tea and wrap up some delicious Grasmere gingerbread. Come back for a hearty cooked breakfast if that suits your plans. We like to show off our local Cumberland sausages and fresh laid eggs from my own hens.'

'That sounds irresistible.'

Eldred answered, the landlady's kindness further cemented his decision to move up to the Fells and lakes of Cumbria. Even the thought of returning down south to Basildon after his holiday felt undesirable now.

The pub began to fill up with more locals and the mysterious men in suits from the ministry, though no one had been told which one. Still craving peace and solitude, Eldred finished his meal and beer and stood up to leave. He walked across to the busy bar ready to thank her but Mrs Graham was on her own serving drinks. He managed to catch her eye with a cheery wave but she abruptly stopped serving a bewildered visitor, hurried away from the bar to take Eldred to one side. Her manner seemed outwardly cheerful but that did not reflect in her eyes that were anxious, unable to meet his.

'The very best place t'camp out is about ten-minute walk from here, a well sheltered spinney facing the beach. Lots of dry firewood and with a little beck running down to sea. Turn sharp left from the pub and keep t' coastal path following the shore line. You can't miss it.'

'Thank you, Mrs Graham, you have been very kind. I will be back for that wonderful breakfast.'

Yes, he really liked Eskscale; he could imagine living in peaceful contentment here.

She watched the offcomer leave, her feelings mixed and at odds with each other. A nice enough man, with eyes that did their best to seem cheerful but could not hide an inner torment. She had seen that look among many local men who survived the war with an essence of them lost forever. If he followed her instructions to the letter, all would be well. Things had quietened down lately, may the bad times never return, but not knowing for sure was a constant source of anxiety of all the old Eskscale families. Word of the officials all the way from London visiting Eskscale had spread throughout the region. Something was up, what with the factory site cleared of every building. The men had also been seen measuring the area and taking notes. Something was most definitely up. Away from the village pub, one individual took a greater interest than most along the gossip highway. Even bad news had an important purpose.

Eldred stood outside the pub and drew in a full lungful of fresh air, the warm breeze scented by the sea and surrounding gorse. So much better than that of the bar of the Herdwick Tup, the aromas of cooked food and beer now overlaid by the stench of pipes, cigarettes and human sweat. He looked left to the coastal path. The beginning of the route was made clear from the lights shining from a row of old stone cottages. A full moon silvered the village rooftops and wind bent trees. The daytime raucous cry of gulls now replaced by the calls of owls and the distant barking of a fox up on the Fells. It was a beautiful night. It would be a shame to waste the ethereal luminosity by having an early night and succumb to fatigue, he had no timetable to keep beyond his own enjoyment. What better time to bathe in the atmosphere of those ancient stones, even if it wasn't his Anglo-Saxon ancestors that built them. A far older people had for their enigmatic, mysterious purposes. It would be a memorable experience, a recollection beyond his pocket book of sketches.

Eldred arrived at the edge of Ryecroft Field and marvelled at the spectacular sight before him. The intensity of the moonlight reflected off the Stones, a bright, silver glow enhanced by sparkling chips of mica within the rock. Behind them in stark contrast, their shadows were dark and sharply delignated. He felt a growing sense of awe and respect for their long dead builders, this creation was both magical and spiritual. Did it matter no one now knew the Circle's purpose, did it even need a purpose beyond its enigmatic, mysterious beauty?

He had to get closer, to touch them, wondering if they gave off an otherworldly vibration. He clambered over the stone wall that surrounded the field with some difficulty, the long day's hiking had begun to stiffen his muscles and re-awaken the still healing, deep pain in his leg. The wall itself was in a pitiful state with broken and loose stones, stray strands of rusty barbed wire. A wide swathe of overgrown briars and stinging nettles in front of it added another line of defence, curiously lush and green compared to the drought wilted plant life beyond the low wall. If there had been a gate to the field, he hadn't seen it, in truth, he was too bewitched to bother to wander along the boundary to find it.

Snagging his clothes and scratching and stinging any exposed skin, Eldred inelegantly scaled the wall, jumping down and landing heavily. He felt a curious movement ripple through the ground. Seismic activity? Surely not in this ancient, settled landscape, it must have been a side effect of his less than graceful descent of the wretched wall. He paused to regain his breath, relaxing as the ground was reassuringly stable and renewing his interest in the Stones with the unpronounceable name. The brightness of the full moon was far better than the single beam of a torch, it bathed the field in silver light and made each Stone stand out in sharp relief. With no overgrown tangle of vegetation to negotiate, Eldred was able to cross the field unhindered, heading for the nearest Standing Stone, his desire to touch its rough-hewn surface overwhelming.

A silent, dark shadow passed through Ryecroft Field, keeping tight behind the moon bathed surfaces of the Stones. Its purpose focused with one intent, to kill and disappear back into the night unseen. This time it would be more cautious, leaving no trace like it had before.

Mrs Graham busied herself cleaning the bar area and

preparing breakfasts, noting the day had dawned bright and warm, promising another scorcher on the way. She would do good business with hot, thirsty locals and any passing tourists seeking a shady respite and cold drinks. She thought again about that pleasant traveller the night before. He seemed so keen to come back to the Tup for breakfast but as the morning lengthened into midday, she hoped he had safely continued his travels.

Two weeks later, other ramblers made a shocking discovery up on the Fells. Decaying quickly from the seeming endless heat, flesh torn to ribbons by scavenging ravens and foxes, the women had found the mortal remains of Henry Eldred. A post mortem revealed he had been totally exsanguinated, not a drop of blood remained in the body or anywhere near it. A curiosity to the coroner. Eldred had been murdered, drained of blood and his body dragged up to the nearest Fell. Not a mystery to Flora Meade and the old Eskscale families. The remains may have been found nowhere near Ryecroft Field, but the connection was too like the dreadful fate of Mrs Smythe to be discounted. Somehow, the Drwg Stones had claimed another victim.

Cleared at last to return to continue the excavation, Stanley was shocked by the increased interest in the Stones, stirred up by word spreading of the second gruesome murder in the area. As the school bus approached Ryecroft field, cars and vans blocked the road, while sight seers traipsed around the ten megaliths, taking photographs. One family had set up a picnic using a stone that had not yet been returned to a standing position, as a table. The bothersome witch and her farmer paramour arrived too but for once they were all in accord. This situation was unacceptable. Stanley stood with his lads by their bus, shaking with growing anger at odds with his once placid nature.

'How can we stop this?'

He hadn't noticed Flora and Jed approach him directly. Her wretched cur, a witch's familiar no doubt had to be held firmly by its collar as it snarled and snapped at Stanley, ignoring her attempts to silence the canine uproar.

'Whisht, Bess, whisht!'

She started to apologise for the dog's unusual behaviour but he waved it aside as unimportant.

'I agree, we must get them off the site immediately,' he shouted above the loud growling. 'I'll go and find Sergeant Brodie. These fools are contaminating a site of priceless scientific importance.'

'These fools are in great danger,' the farmer muttered, confirming Stanley's opinion, this was a superstitious buffoon of a local, 'this site should have been left untouched.'

The school boy excavation team had wandered off their coach and stood by the wall to watch their site overrun by offcomers. Most found the invasion amusing and jeered at the visitors. Others hoped the strangers gave an excuse for not having to dig in the drowsy summer heat and inevitable rock-hard ground. One lad stood back from the others, trying to distance himself from the field. Freddie Adams. He glanced across to Flora, a look of desperation on his face ashen despite a summer kissed tan. With the school master stomping off to find the authority to clear the field, Freddie broke away unnoticed by the other boys and hurried across to Flora.

'Something bad is going to happen, I can feel

darkness stirring in the ground around the Stones.'

Flora put her arm around the lad, who was shivering despite the relentlessly hot sun. How she wished she could take him home with her, let him become part of her family. He would be free to voice his concerns openly, be taught to protect himself from his own abilities. To feel safe and loved for who he was and not who he pretended to be.

'What is this darkness you feel, Freddie? You know I will believe you however strange it may be.'

The boy wiped away tears of gratitude, he was not a freak to be mocked and jostled to the woman with the red hair and marvellous golden eyes.

'Anger, a vast, hidden fury rising from unimaginable depths. '

Freddie's eyes had become unfocused, his words spoken in a strange, flat voice. He was channelling someone or something not of this world. Flora groaned in disappointment as Stanley was already returning from the village with Sergeant Brodie. She needed to know more but the boy was out of his trance and scurrying back to the excavation team. Freddie had told her all the boys had been warned not to speak to the villagers, in particular the crazy red headed woman who thinks she is a witch. Flora understood the lad's dilemma, best he was not seen with her now.

A high-pitched scream pierced the uneasy calm. A woman ran across the uneven ground, an arcing spray of blood from a deep, arterial wound in her wrist. Without a pause, Flora ran to help her. It was the first time she had ever set foot in the field and the assault on her body and mind was immediate. Jed caught her as she dropped to the ground, overwhelmed by waves of alien emotions of deep fury and overwhelming contempt. Fortunately, others also ran to aid the injured woman. The ground beneath them surged as if the soil covered a monstrous, angry beast. Jed swept Flora into his arms, fighting to keep his balance as he ran across the swaying, bucking earth back to the field boundary. A glance across to the road showed that the land beyond the field remained still and solid. Spectators on the road were not being thrown about but standing still, confusion and shock on their faces.

There was no need of Sergeant Brodie's help ridding the Ryecroft site of unwanted offcomers. The field had shaken them off like a dog ridding itself of fleas. The injured woman had left with her companions, rushing her to the nearest hospital. Flora sat on the grass bank opposite the field, recovering while Jed helped the sergeant calm the picnickers, doing their best to reassure them that the land beyond the field was stable and safe. Freddie used the confusion to return to Flora. She gave the boy, shivering from fear a tight hug. He found strength and reassurance from embrace but kept his back to the cursed field. Flora tried to reassure him.

'Everyone is out of there and safe now, the lady with the injured arm will recover.'

'But safe for how long, Mrs Meade?

Once again, the boy's voice changed, the sense that he was channelling some old but human presence.

'The fury deep below has been awakened. If the warning is unheeded, the horrors will spread beyond these Guardian stones. Unstoppable horrors.'

He blinked, momentarily confused, shaking off whatever had taken over his voice. He had no recollections of what had just passed.

Flora held out her arms and took his arms in a light grip, 'Freddie, you are a part of something greater and older despite being so young. But you are not alone, far from it. My family is now your family. You will always find love, hope and protection from us and Jed.

She gave his arms a firmer squeeze.

'Remember that, we are here for you … always.'

Before he could answer, he heard his name called by the schoolboy leader of the young excavators.

'I have to go, Mrs Meade.'

Freddie ran back to the others who were hurriedly shepherded onto their coach, the startled driver revving the engine, eager to be back to the sanity of the school. To the driver's irritation, their teacher seemed to be in a daze, wandering over in an unhurried pace with frequent glances back at the Stones. Once on board he signalled the driver to proceed, without doing the routine head count of lads or even checking if anyone had been injured in the mayhem.

Yet more blood had been spilt, a spattering of fresh red against the sparse, yellow grass and the sombre grey of the Stones. It would soon be lost from sight, every drop absorbed by the earth and the Stones and leaving no trace. Something Stanley found deeply pleasing. The bloodshed had quietened the clamour and barrage of voices in his mind to a quieter but endless whisper. A welcome lull before the strident demands began again.

5

Autumn 1949

It had been a good night's work, Ed Thwaite's burlap bag heavy with three brace of fat pheasants poached from Lord Tedborough's shooting estate. He had buyers lined up already for the plump game birds. Madge, his wife refused to have stolen dead things hanging in their coal shed, let alone in the house. They needed the income though, with work scarce since the munitions factory closed, as was what little was left of the money the newspapers paid his lads for their gruesome story. With no sense of irony, Thwaite first believed discovering the mangled body of that crazy old offcomer woman had been a godsend to the Thwaites. Sadly, a short lived one as the reporters disappeared overnight to chase another lurid story that would sell newspapers. Some high up Tory MP found in Cornwall in woman's clothing apparently.

He walked alone under a bright, full moon, shining on autumn leaves skittering across the road. Alone apart from his long dog, Grum, the creature's dark grey, shaggy coat silvered by the moonlight. A good working dog apart from its idiocy getting past Ryecroft field. Cursing, he always had to drag the whimpering cur by the wide leather collar past it. Fortunately, last time it did this, the lurcher had recovered enough to bring down a big buck hare to add to that night's bounty. He had insisted Kate cooked it: a man brought home good food for his wife to feed the bairns with. That was how it should be.

Once again, Thwaite faced passing Ryecroft with the Stones, silent watchmen with long, deep shadows under the cold, indifferent moon. He felt no sense of unease or fear of this creepy sight, the work of long dead and mysterious ancestors. Stones were just that, rough-hewn lumps of old rock. The frightening stories passed down the generations, no more than useful ways to make bairns behave. Those tales had not worked on his two older lads. Bloody-minded like their father, he too had been a tearaway at their age. Readjusting the heavy bag of poached game, Thwaite thought with a chuckle that the locals rightly believed he still was.

Grum fell to the ground, its whole-body quivering, a low keening of terror vibrating from its throat. Not this nonsense again. Thwaite tugged at the lurcher's lead, kicked at the dog's backside and ribs to no avail. Something moved at the periphery of the poacher's vision, a swift, black and sinuous shadow. Too big to be any creature, perhaps too thin to be a man. He lessened his tight grip on the dog, too engrossed in this mystery to notice it bolting away in the opposite direction.

Moving back from the centre of the road, Thwaite stood in the shade of a yew tree, away from the brightness of the moonlight. He saw the shadow again, the moonbeams shining between the Stones not adding to any clarity to what the damned thing was. It appeared again, slinking around the field as if searching out prey. It tried to keep out of the moonlight and stay in the long shadows behind the Stones but it was far darker, its shape an intense black making it possible to see it.

Thwaite bit down hard on his gnarled hands to stifle a scream, it had no face. Unable to move, he sunk to the ground, curled up in a tight foetal position. If he tried to bolt away like the dog, the fiend would surely spot him and overwhelm him. All his life he'd dismissed and ignored the old warnings about the Drood Men. Now he faced being ripped apart like those offcomers. That interfering old biddy had it coming but he'd done nothing wrong. Anger rose above his fear yet he had the sense to stay beneath the yew.

At some point, he must have succumbed to sleep. Heavy rain arrived with the dawn and it woke him up, still curled on the dry ground beneath the tree. His body cold, his limbs stiff and cramped, he made his way home. Thwaite tried to pass the whole experience off as a bad dream but couldn't shake off the truth. He had seen one of the Drood Men and lived. He would say nothing though. He has an image to protect as a tough man, a no-nonsense type, people would think he was tapped in the head ranting on about a shadowy monster. Or angering the old-time villagers again by selling his story to the sensation-seeking press. He'd taken enough flak over the boys' story splashed over the papers. He'd explain his late arrival home to the missus by telling her that the dog had run off and he'd spent the night searching for the idiotic cur. It was probably home already, curled up by the kitchen range, being spoiled by his wife. Thwaite's night spent cowering under a yew tree never happened.

With no further horrors, it seemed the terrible deaths of Geraldine Smythe and the tourist Henry Eldred had been isolated incidents. The work of a lone maniac, perhaps a drifter from outside the area. Why they had been targeted remained unknown, everything about the

Stones was a mystery. The incident with the tourists was put down to a small though strangely localised earthquake and deliberately forgotten. Flora had not let down her guard, even as village life returned to a form of wary normality. The cursed field still belonged to the absentee landowner who stubbornly refused to sell it, no matter how much money the villagers had raised. All the negotiations were done through the owner's solicitors, so nobody knew why the titleholder remained so intransient. Without the mysterious owner's permission, the locals agreed one precaution. Using high banks of earth, they sealed up a footpath that ran from the main road and alongside Ryecroft Field. No one from the village ever used it and closing it might deter any unwary offcomer tourist from hiking along it.

Despite the gradual return of calm to the community, the horrific deaths had cemented underlying fears and kept the rumour mill turning. Flora considered this a good thing, hopefully it might keep adventurous village children and thrill-seeking young people from danger. Occasionally a local passing swiftly by the Stones along the nearby lane spoke of a single eerie shadow flitting around the monument but nothing more than that tenuous suggestion of unnatural activity. Keeping a journal, Flora recorded every mention of shadows with meticulous care, trying to find a pattern, a trigger that could provoke it or them into action. One thing was certain, they may appear to be just eerie shadows, a trick of the light and vivid imaginations, but this phenomenon was potentially lethal. She knew that violent disturbance of the ground was not an earthquake but an unnatural occurrence. A stirring of unimaginable power.

Flora's research into the field's history had yielded

little of use. It had belonged to the same local family for many hundreds of years, historically fascinating but a dead end. When the last heir to the farm passed away, the farm was broken up and sold off in parcels of land. The Ryecroft paddock had been retained, and let out to a succession of short-term tenants. It appeared that all considered it unfarmable. The last letting began and ended in 1820.

With Rev. Winter's willing help, she also studied the parish records with no greater luck. That there was something malign about the field and its once hidden Stones was clearly a local legend preserved only in oral form, passed down from countless centuries. Though she was unhappy about upsetting them, Flora had quizzed Eskscale's eldest inhabitants, in particular Mrs Blamire, at ninety-three, the old lady's mind was still pin sharp, her memories lucid. Once a village school mistress, there was little about old Eskscale, Nellie Blamire didn't know.

Flora chose a time when she knew Rowan and Ash would be at school. Her attempts at protecting them from her near obsessive search for the truth about the Stones seemed to be working. Though lately, Rowen's knowing witch-to-be-eyes spoke of the girl's awareness of the situation. Deep down, her mother with a surge of pride, sensed Rowan was going to be a formidable wise woman in the future. A future, it was her mother's duty to protect. Now Flora was just relieved the children had not had bad nightmares or seemed unhappy and had openly laughed off the wilder rumours inevitably circulating in the school playground. They enjoyed their mother's extra attempts at spending fun time with them, the picnics, kite flying along the beach, the trips by train into Whitehaven to catch a new Disney film.

With the children safely occupied, Flora had made her way to speak to Nellie Blamire. Taking some home-baked soft ginger biscuits and a bottle of elderflower and blackberry cordial, she walked to the little terraced home a couple of streets away from hers. The old lady seemed relieved to talk openly about the old legends. Flora got her settled in front of her hearth with a fresh cup of tea and made the old lady comfortable with a patchwork blanket over her knees.

Nellie Blamire was fiercely independent despite her great age but had reluctantly accepted help from the community and another victim of the past war, her widowed niece by marriage, Lottie, who now lived permanently with her. Flora had promised the younger woman she would stay with Nellie for the afternoon, giving the niece a chance to get the train to Whitehaven to get her hair done and catch a film. She had taken little persuasion, rushing off to catch 'So Long at the Fair' with that dashing Dirk Bogarde and pretty Jean Simmons with a rare smile of anticipation on her homely face. Such rare diversions were there to be savoured.

With the niece considered an offcomer, the old lady relaxed and opened up once she had left, knowing however far-fetched the story may seem, the latest generation of Eskscale wise woman would believe her.

'The Stones were not always covered up, you know,' Nellie announced as she divulged her knowledge between sips of tea, 'there was a time when they stood as proud as those at Castlerigg.'

Flora knew those ones well, they were a wonder of the Fells near Keswick, in a beautiful setting and imbued with a magical aura of romance and mystery. She always felt energised, revived in their midst. There couldn't have been a greater contrast with Eskscale's ominous ancient circle.

'Proud but not right,' Nellie continued, 'there was nothing sacred to our ancestors with those old Stones. People and animals alike shunned them. Occasionally a villager or visiting fisherman would be found dead … head twisted off like that poor woman last year. They earned their old name, "The Drwg Circle".'

'In the end, a local *yacker* had enough. Named Nathan Hart, a widower I believe. Lost his only son to the Drood Men. Poor child fell, cracked his skull open on one of the Stones. What worse could befall that poor father? Hart toiled like a man possessed, not stopping until every stone was deep beneath the earth.'

Flora pondered over the strange term 'Drood man.' She only knew it as a local term to scare naughty children to eat their supper or go to bed. Foolishly, she had never connected it to Ryecroft. Thought it no more than a traditional Cumberland scare story like the Lakeland Tizzie Wizzie or the Screaming Skulls of Calgarth Hall.

'How long ago was this, Nellie?'

The old lady laughed, showing a surprising number of still good, white teeth, 'Oh my, now you are asking! In the aald days, that's for sure. I remember my aald grandpa telling me when I was nobbut knee high 'til a goose.'

Not wanting to press her or interrupt her train of thought, Flora waited patiently for the woman to talk again, Nelly was enjoying a change of company and the biscuits, still warm from the oven, dunked in her tea.

'Always interested in history, I was as a lass, still am now, even if I am part of it for the young 'uns. I'd have loved to have known more but that was all my grandpa told me … that and to beware of the Drood Men if the

Stones were ever to see the light of day again.'

Again, that strange term. Flora leant forward and took the woman's cold, frail hands, the bird-like bones so close to the paper-thin skin.

'These Drood Men, did your grandpa tell you who or what they were?'

Nelly sat back in her chair, her already pale face blanching.

'He did and I wish he hadn't. Not with those offcomers digging up what should stay below the earth. They are not men ... the Drood are fiends. The name comes from the Welsh for dark or evil ... "*drwg*". Similar to our old Cumberland language lost to time and the wretched Saxon offcomers.'

Pausing, Nellie leant closer to her guest.

'They are the guardians of a burial ground of some terrible aald monster. Leave 'em alone and no harm will come to us in Eskscale.'

She sighed and gazed into Flora's eyes. 'But some folk will never leave things alone, will they? Not with offcomers moving to the village all the time, ignoring our aald legends and bringing death.'

Flora could see this talk of monsters was upsetting the old woman and after giving her a hug, walked over to the range and brewed fresh tea. To Nellie's relief, her visitor changed the subject; there was always plenty of gossip to reveal with a knowing smile and a wink. By the time her niece returned with newly permed hair and a sparkle in her eyes from sighing over Dirk Bogarde, Nellie appeared to be back to her cheery self. But as Flora said her goodbyes, the old woman grabbed her hand and pulled her down to whisper.

'This is now time to be what you were born for, witch woman. You must be strong, learn all you can because them creatures won't just go away now.

After her talk with old Mrs Blamire, Flora could not accept the wall of silence and mute acceptance from the unofficial Eskscale 'elders' anymore. If they knew something about the so called Drood Men, this was time to share it. If it was genuinely nothing but an eccentric old boogie man legend, then she needed to know that, to find out what really was so wrong and threatening from the Ryecroft stone circle. Whether there was a deranged killer on the loose, some sort of mentally disturbed cultist using the Stones as a symbolic focus. After her last, brief chat with young Freddie Adams, her thoughts tended towards the supernatural.

When Jed had first brought the boy to her cottage that spring, the lad had stayed long enough to calm down, have a good tea, dry off and find solace and comfort with her family and Jed. Flora had learned from Freddie that he was an unwanted orphan and she knew that his gift would always leave him vulnerable. Perhaps her cottage could stretch to another youngster under its protective roof?

6

It took patience and a determined refusal to be fobbed off, but Flora had finally tracked down some details of the elusive owner of Ryecroft field. It was not their actual name, but that of the land agents dealing with any matters concerning the field. It was frustrating that she could only communicate through his or her London solicitors but now Flora found herself in a busy, smoky carriage pulled by the Duchess of Sutherland locomotive on route to London. Progress of sorts.

Keeping a tight grip on the bamboo handles of her carpet bag for dubious comfort, Flora was nervous, she had never been further south than Blackburn and never to a city as large as the capital. She gazed out of the window, saw the passing countryside through the wafts of thick sooty steam and wondered what she would find at the Kensington offices of Greene, Knightly and Barnes, solicitors.

She was only an hour into her journey south but was already missing Rowan and Ash, the centre of her universe. The children were being spoilt rotten, staying with their cousins in Whitehaven. Flora would never have left them back in Eskscale without her protection. Indeed, she had many times considered sending them to stay with Ada, her sister-in-law, her husband Leo and their boisterous but lovable three children on a more permanent basis while the danger from the lethal shadows existed. She had considered suggesting all the village children should be evacuated if the creatures from the Stones killed again. The older families, especially those with children would understand. Newcomers would think her crazy. So they remained with their mother under her anxious, protective care.

Her mind was increasingly conflicted and confused these days but at no point did she consider leaving Eskscale, however tempting the thought. She had been raised by her mother to understand and accept her duties and however daunting, she would not turn away from them.

Nothing prepared her for the capital, when countryside gave way to new built leafy suburbs then to grime-encrusted, tightly packed terraces and smoky factories. London was huge, impersonal and overcrowded. She got off the train at Euston and stood on the forecourt as hundreds of people pushed past, heads down, all in a frenzied hurry. So lost in their haste, Flora was jostled many times with only an occasional mumbled apology. She made her way outside the station and fumbled in her handbag for the address she sought. Flora had been warned London taxi drivers knew their city like the back of their hand but were expensive, she hoped she had enough to reach Kensington.

A cheery cockney driver chatted throughout the seemingly interminable journey across London, nothing but stop and start, jams and diversions. Cars, lorries, buses and horse drawn delivery carts jostled for space with the black London cabs. It was chaotic and Flora was heartened that this was just a fleeting visit; she would not have to live here in this toxic fume–laden mayhem. The cab pulled up outside a Georgian townhouse off Kensington High Street, a gracious building that once housed a well to do family, but now converted to offices. To her relief, the cab fare was reasonable and the cabbie helped her by writing down how to make a connection to her train home by underground trains, much cheaper and quicker for the out-of-town traveller. Good folk could be found everywhere.

She was greeted with aloof politeness by a female clerk and taken to a waiting room.

'Young Mr Barnes will see you shortly, he is just finishing with an important client.'

Flora was aware of the deliberate emphasis on the word 'important', that the clerk was putting this northern nobody in her place. She ignored the rudeness. She would have welcomed a cup of tea, or even a glass of water after her long journey but unsurprisingly, none was offered. Not all Londoners were like the friendly cabby it seemed. She hoped Young Mr Barnes was more pleasant and forthcoming. After an hour, she had slipped into despondency, no one was interested in her, perhaps she had even been forgotten by Miss Frosty Knickers in the outer office. She was just about to walk out when the door opened and an elderly gentleman held out his hand to her. 'Profuse apologies, Mrs Meade, most unacceptable. I had a most difficult case to deal with, a distraught, recently widowed lady with a complicated and disputed estate.'

'How distressing,' Flora murmured, shaking the man's bony, gnarled hand, 'There is no need to apologise.'

Young Mr Barnes must have been eighty at least. Old enough at least to have some useful knowledge of the history of Ryecroft Field.

'I hope Miss Simmons looked after you during your tiring journey and vexing long wait.'

'Actually, no, I would be grateful for a glass of water.'

Flora had no qualms about getting the clerk in

trouble, some people brought it on themselves.

'My dear lady, let me take you to lunch, there is nothing we cannot discuss over good food.'

A short walk to the High Street brought them to a restaurant, where Flora was grateful for the hot meal of a hearty beef stew full of potatoes and carrots followed by a steamed treacle pudding with thick, creamy custard, all washed down with freshly brewed tea. Her rushed, pre-dawn breakfast of toast and scrape seemed an eternity ago. At last, Flora felt relaxed and comfortable enough with the old man's affable company to pursue her quest. As if to further put her at ease, Barnes spoke first,

'Researching your request has certainly been fascinating for me. What was a routine and dull search through dusty old files has become enlivened with a certain air of mystery.'

'Did you know, for instance, back in the ninth century, some intrepid Norse raiders came ashore, finding the immediate area curiously empty of settlements. An odd fact considering the farming and fishing opportunities there and the natural haven to shelter their long ships. They were the ones who named your village.'

Flora nodded, though nothing about her village had seemed normal to her for a very long time. She waited until Barnes replenished their tea cups and listened to his enthusiastic discourse.

'The ancient Stones were already in place and primeval, built and named Drwg by the ancestors of the native Brythonic tribes living in the surrounding area. The Norse settlers of the time had respect for the old gods of the indigenous people they now lived among and left the Stones untouched. Unperturbed by the presence of the Drwg Stones, the Norse did settle on the flat land by the Irish Sea. They called their village Eskskali, meaning a wooden shelter by a river.'

'How fascinating,' Flora interrupted, it was the more recent history she wanted to learn about, 'but who owns the land on which the Drwg Stones stand now? I was hoping I could meet the new owner of the field. From what was said in your firm's letter to me.'

'Really?'

Barnes looked flustered, caught off guard.

'I am so sorry, there must have been some misunderstanding. The gentleman has no wish to discuss this matter in person with anyone. Or release his name or whereabouts.'

Sinking back in her seat, Flora's mind went back to that horrible clerk, maybe she had engineered this fool's errand out of some twisted sense of amusement. She pushed away an impulse to hex Miss Simmons, such negativity had a way of backfiring and decided to learn all she could from the affable Barnes.

'We are a well-established firm, Mrs Meade, founded in 1870. We took over the Kensington building and many existing cases including this one from Abercrombie's, an exceedingly old company of lawyers and land agents. Ryecroft Field was once owned by one wealthy Cumberland family over many generations, part of a widespread estate administered from their ancestral home in Calderbridge. Now mainly broken up and sold on, they kept Ryecroft Field in the family but once let it out to tenant farmers. They no longer make it possible to rent though. Or purchase. '

'Calderbridge,' Flora murmured out loud to herself, why did this seem important? It was an area inland, not far from Eskscale. Apologising for the interruption, she urged Barnes to continue.

'In 1420, a tenant farmer named Nathan Fox buried all but of the Stones, without the permission of the landowner. This was considered a welcome move by all accounts, the locals made no protest, though the owning family was outraged. There was quite an unpleasant scene when the owner himself arrived with an army of labourers to uncover the Stones. The villagers outnumbered them and sent them packing.'

Flora remembered the old lady's story, of how Nathan Fox was driven by grief to bury the Stones. Nellie believed a time of peace had fallen on the village after his action. There had been no talk of digging them up until the arrival of the excavation team of school boys.

'Can you tell me where the landowning family were from in Calderbridge?'

Barnes drained his tea cup and paused. Was this a breach of confidence? He sighed before answering. This determined young woman could easily find out by visiting the village, so close to her own. What harm could it do?

'The family moved away from Cumberland a long time ago. They once lived in Fellview House, Ponsonby.'

Flora shivered, suddenly cold despite the steamy fug of the packed restaurant. Fellview, now where the school lads excavating the Stones came from. Coincidence? In her world of mysterious ancient ley lines and so many other esoteric connections, true coincidences were rare.

'Now, if I may,' Barnes looked uncomfortable, 'I would be interested in why you are so interested in a small, commonplace field. Are you interested in letting or buying it? I hear Eskscale maybe in line for somewhat of a revival of fortune. It could be a wise investment.'

'Possibly, we already have a cooperative of sorts, local folk who want to pool their resources to buy Ryecroft.'

Barnes looked unsurprised.

'Indeed, our firm has a weighty file of all the past requests, all refused as you know.'

'Don't you find that odd, Mr Barnes?' Flora ventured, finishing her tea, her spirits sinking. Was this as far as she could get?

'In the past, yes,' he agreed, 'but now with the proposed developments of the area, it would be a wise move to hold on to the highest price. With all due respect, I suspect that the best price would come from Her Majesty's Government and not a collection of local villagers.'

This was the first time she had heard of any government interest in Eskscale and its surrounds since the war. As usual it seems, the locals were the last to know. But most rumour mills ran fast and false, she would only tell the others their bid to buy the field would be refused.

7

Winter 1949

The Fellview team had finished their excavation, leaving the site to historians to measure and photograph the Stones and finds. Then they too left Eskscale and an uneasy peace returned to the relieved community. At least there was joyous celebration when Jed and Flora were married in the parish church by Rev. Wilson and attended by all the old Eskscale family villagers. That night the happy couple held a simple, heartfelt pagan hand fasting ceremony at Jed's farm, their new home. This one only attended by Rowan and Ash, Nellie Blamire and the family's many pets.

The mutual desire to adopt Freddie Adams sadly wasn't to be. Flora and Jed had made an appointment with Arthur Robley, the headmaster of Fellview School once they were officially married and deemed respectable enough. As they walked through the dark, oak panelled corridors of the converted Victorian mansion, Flora shuddered at many reminders of the disastrous excavation at Eskscale. On the walls were proudly displayed photographs of each stage of the dig, and images of the lads including Freddie's pale, haunted face.

'Unfortunately, the developing process went a bit awry with many of these images,' explained Robley, 'the wild weather conditions of your locale perhaps?'

Flora examined them closer, feeling oddly faint at the

sight of her old adversary, Mr Stanley. Jed saw the same thing and put a supporting arm around her shoulders. Images taken on sunny days showed each lad with a shadow proportionate to his height. Not so their teacher, every image of Stanley had multiple, elongated dark shadows surrounding him, all snake-like and taller than him. The schoolboy photographer had unwittingly captured an image of the Drood. Still shaking from the revelation, the Barrows were shown into the headmaster's office and offered tea, which they accepted.

'A stiff brandy would be better,' Jed muttered to his wife, once Robley left them to arrange it, 'seeing them beggars on photos is enough to flaiten away any man's wits.'

The headmaster returned, followed by a schoolboy carrying a wooden tray with tea things, the school's hospitality did not extend to biscuits. Robley waited until his guests were served before addressing them from behind an overlarge oak desk.

'I am afraid you are here on a fool's errand, Mr and Mrs Barrows. But I thought anyone generous enough to offer a home to one of our tearaways deserved to be told in person. Freddie Adams is no longer at Fellview. He has run away.'

Robley waited while the would-be parents absorbed the news.

'Absconding is a common enough occurrence among boys in approved schools. We do not run prisons; this is not a Borstal for young offenders.'

Wiping away tears, Flora did her best to overcome her anger, how could a vulnerable young boy be allowed to leave a place of safety and not be found by the authorities?

'Did you even bother to look for him? I see by your face you did not. What about the master who supervised the excavation? Does Mr Stanley know what happened, where Freddie may have gone? The boy knew we would welcome him as part of our family, why would he have run away?'

'Mr Stanley left our employ a few weeks later, I believe he missed the bustle of his former life down in London but he did not leave a forwarding address or request references. Odd, but maybe he had enough of teaching difficult and troubled pupils. Or came into money? His family were believed to be wealthy.'

The journey back to Eskscale was a sad one with such distressing news for the Barrows, never had the Fells in winter felt so bleak. Sleet and rain lashed Jed's Land Rover as the winds from the Irish Sea battered in vain against its sturdy metal sides.

'We'll find him, lass.' Jed soothed, his voice determined.

Flora did not answer. Maybe they had been the true cause of the lad's flight. With Freddie's occult special Sight, she understood why the lad would want to steer well clear of The Stones. Perhaps they had been too selfish and insensitive to think he would ever be happy in Eskscale, knowing what haunted it. All she could do was hang onto hope, that one day the lad would find a way back to them. He would always be welcomed into their family. Always.

The uneasy calm did not last long for Eskscale. Centuries had ignored the village, for so long no more than hamlet of fisher folk and farmers. A brief flirtation by intrepid Victorians to turn it into a seaside resort had left a legacy of the small, coastal railway and the picturesque Eskscale station but little else. But not the Twentieth. The remote setting that had made it an ideal site for a wartime munitions works, also earmarked it for another purpose. One that did not sit so easily on the inhabitants.

Shortly after Flora's futile trip south, a government deputation had arrived from London and held a meeting for all Eskscale residents and those from surrounding farms. Their mission was to explain the need for a nuclear power plant on the munition site and to allay any understandable fears the locals would have. With great enthusiasm, they preached a new scientific gospel, of an exciting age of safe, clean power that would benefit the whole country. There would be boffins of course and skilled engineers, many looking for homes in the area for their families but there would be no shortage of employment for the locals.

The officials pinned up their proposals and maps of the development, called Brathay Power Plant and retired to leave the villagers alone to discuss the scheme. A well-respected local man, David Anson spoke out.

'This is good news. At least we will have work coming to the area, plenty of it, too.'

Many at the village hall meeting murmured and nodded their agreement at Anson's words. A young father with a wife and three-year-old son, a decent, hard-working man, safely back from the war but reduced like so many, to scratching around for any odd jobs to put bread on the table.

'I second that,' shouted Ed Thwaite, 'just what we need, an honest day's work and the government paying us for it. As long as they don't hand it all out to offcomers.'

The local rascal's words raised a few stifled laughs

from the villagers, his dodgy reputation all too well known. Glancing across the small, packed hall, Flora caught Rev Winters' eye and saw the deep concern clouding his thoughts. Anxieties she shared.

How could Flora argue against the power plant and disrespect the hopes of these Eskscale men? The chance to remain in their home village and make a decent living? Yet how could the thought of the disused wartime munitions works at Eskscale being rebuilt as a nuclear power plant not fill her with dismay? Human beings holding the power of gods to destroy the world and that energy created so close to the site of a much older, unknown power. Madness, but no amount of warning could change this happening. As a mother she feared for her children's future. As a wise woman she feared for the future of the planet. At least she had her husband at her side, Jed was the man who loved her and the children and believed her fears. He was her rock.

It was clear from their expressions that some members of the old Eskscale families shared her unspoken concerns and conflicting views of this development. There had been no problems from Ryecroft field while the war time munition factory had functioned and new work in the area was desperately needed. But that was before that damn fool uncovered the Stones. With a heavy heart, and a mind full of conflict, Flora chose to keep silent.

8

Eskscale, 1954

Rhys Jones drove his trusty rose taupe Morris Minor along the coast road towards his new life. The late summer morning, already warm with a balmy breeze off the Irish Sea lifted his spirits and he belted out his favourite songs from musicals, heard only by the swooping overhead gulls and indifferent sheep in the flat fields of yellowed grass. This was a mercy as he was that rare Welshman who would be drummed out of any choir for being tone deaf.

One of a new breed of nuclear scientists, Jones had travelled from his London University post to be part of the team creating Brathay, Britain's first power station to provide electricity for the population. That it would also provide nuclear fuel for weapons had caused him much soul searching. He reasoned the world was no less dangerous despite the end of the war, perhaps Britain would be safer defended by those hellish creations of scientists. Weapons created with unwilling help by people like him.

With most of the sign posts still not replaced after the wartime precautions, Jones followed his instincts to find Eskscale, keeping to the coastal road should in theory lead directly to what was once a sleepy, coastal village. Plans to build the nuclear plant were advancing swiftly, aided by a supportive local population, the men desperate for work, any work that could put food on their family's table. Newcomers like Jones, the scientists and engineers, many with families were also moving to Eskscale and surrounds.

Blessed now by the muted hues of late summer and benevolent warm sunshine, Jones knew this was a rare moment of calm and peace. The region's weather was not always so benign, as when mighty gales blew across from the Irish Sea or snow storms straight down from the Arctic. This was a remote, windswept place, hemmed in by the mighty Fells of the Lake District and an often stormy and unpredictable sea. The Ministry knew what they were doing in choosing this sparsely populated location.

For Jones, the isolation could be problematical. It had caused him some sleepless nights after accepting the well-paid post. Born and raised in central Cardiff, studying and then working in London, he liked being in the centre of things, friendly pubs, theatres and cinemas. Other people to relax with after days spent wrestling with complex mathematics and dangerous elements. What would his life be like here? There was just the one pub, and that frequented by rough-hewn fishermen and shepherds. He was a twenty-five-year-old single man, not bad looking by all accounts, with windswept black hair and green eyes and the soulful face of a young Welsh bard. But even chatting to a pretty lass could infuriate some local swain. This remote, rural setting was a foreign land to Jones, a minefield of differing attitudes and customs.

Pushing aside such idle thoughts, Jones pulled around a narrow bend to see the village below him. He parked on stony verge and got out of the car to stretch after the hours behind the wheel and take in his new home, breathing in the salty, invigorating air. The calm sea sparkled like green glass, there was a long, narrow sandy beach against which some Victorian buildings huddled together as if for support. A coastal railway snaked alongside the sea front, also built by the enterprising and optimistic Victorians. Clusters of new homes had sprung up along the edge of the village, many more in the early stages of construction. Eskscale was swiftly on its way to becoming a small town with the influx of newcomers like himself. Jones pondered again on the welcome this once close-knit community would give him.

Inevitably, his gaze went beyond Eskscale itself and on to a dark mass a mile inland but looking far closer, a gouged out ugly scar on the surrounding landscape of green fields. The size of the works and edifices already dwarfed the village, in particular the four cooling towers that already dominated the skyline and were visible for miles around. He decided to take a detour past the works, what would be the central focus of his life from tomorrow morning.

He passed a gaggle of local children, towels tucked under their arms walking towards the beach, all smiled and waved at him. He returned the cheery greetings with a wave and smile. A good sign. Perhaps strangers were not treated with suspicion and hostility here.

Something unexpected caught his attention and once again, Jones found somewhere to park and left the car. In the lee of the Brathay works, in a scruffy field stood a circle of ten standing stones. Fascinated by ancient history, he crossed the road and leant against the field's surrounding wall. His beloved Welsh homeland was full of such enigmatic early monuments to ancient beliefs, though his city upbringing didn't bring him into contact with any. What drove those people to toil so hard excavating these mammoth lumps of rock, to shape them with stone and antler tools and drag them far across a mountainous landscape without roads to this particular location? To honour the passing of a great leader? To fulfil some vital religious purpose? There was talk of these mysterious circles being astronomical devices charting the positions of sunrise, the moon and stars.

Jones shivered. He glanced up at the sky, expecting a fleeting cloud covering the sun but the blue remained uninterrupted by nothing bigger than a passing seagull. Without knowing why, he stepped back from the wall around the field. Every nerve end seemed to screaming at him, urging him to flee. But from what?

Determined not to be spooked by an idiotic, inexplicable sensation, Jones held his ground, glancing back across the prehistoric monument. There was something unwanted and neglected about the Stones. Nothing had been done to cut back the untidy tangle of nettles and dense clumps of thistles around their bases. Lichen and moss grew from every crack and crevice on their coarse surfaces. Yet they stood, powerful in their mute defiance of the desecration by nature. Shadows moved among them, shades that did not belong anywhere but in a nightmare. A ridiculous notion, Jones swallowed hard, bracing himself to turn his back on the field and return to his car. He tried to stay calm and walk but by the time he reached the Morris Minor, he was running.

Unsettled by something he could not explain to himself, let alone anyone else, he drove at speed to the village, parking at the Seaview hotel. It was a stolid Victorian red brick building, built in that brief time of optimism, in the forlorn hope Eskscale could become a flourishing holiday resort. Something had prevented the village's growth and prosperity despite its clearly fine beach and charming views of the surrounding Fells. Whatever that was had not turned up in Jones' initial library researches into the area he was to now call home.

At least, with the building of Brathay, the hotel finally enjoyed its first real prosperity and Jones was made welcome as soon as he entered the mahogany panelled reception. A cheery porter with a hard-to-understand local accent took his bags up to a comfortable if somewhat old-fashioned bedroom. It had pleasing sea views and spotlessly clean, though well-worn, linen on a well-sprung bed. The young scientist was still shaken by the Stones and decided he preferred the company of strangers to his own. After freshening up, he went downstairs to seek out the hotel bar and lounge.

He bought a pint of a local brew and found a comfortable seat. The hotel lounge was busy, he recognised London and Manchester accents around him and before long he was joined by a young couple.

'I take it you are one of the new boffins?'

Holding out his hand, a bluff, sandy-haired man, about ten years older than Jones introduced himself, 'Craig, Gerard Craig, technician. I oversee the cooling systems. This lovely lady is *Dr* Jean Sherrington, something to do with those mysterious atoms you guys mess about with.'

Jean Sherrington was an attractive woman in her late thirties, despite doing all she could to hide her looks. Her hair was tightly drawn back in a severe bun, and she wore heavy framed spectacles and no makeup. It didn't work, if anything it drew more attention to her high cheekbones and deep grey eyes.

'Rhys Jones? The boy genius of particle science?' she ventured with a warm smile. 'Your reputation over research with isometric transmissions goes before you.'

'As does yours, Dr Sherrington,' he replied, more than a little awestruck, 'I've read all your papers on secular equilibrium.'

'Then you are misspending the fleeting years of your youth, Mr Jones,' she said with the ghost of a smile. 'Far too much time with your nose buried in some dry and boring treatise of mine.'

Craig laughed and slapped his hand down on the wooden table, 'then we must do all we can to fix that.'

He stood up and rubbed his hands together. 'So, let's have no more work talk from you brain box nuclear physicists. The bar will be closing any minute, so let's enjoy what's left of our Sunday off and get right royally plastered.'

Smiling, Jones walked across to the bar with the technician. He had only been in Eskscale for an hour and had already made contact with fellow newcomers. Memories of that tangled field and the shadowed Stones faded but were not forgotten.

The next morning began well. Another glorious day dawned with the early morning sun gilding a calm brown and green glass sea and the evocative cries of seabirds. As he washed and dressed, Jones smelled the enticing waft of bacon cooking from the hotel kitchens. He went down stairs with a pleasing sense of anticipation for the first day of his new posting.

Jones was treated to a hearty cooked breakfast in the company of other workers from the plant staying at the hotel. He didn't speak beyond what was required to be polite, he preferred to listen, to learn as much as he could. Any problems, any grievances or difficult managers to be wary of, but the talk was all light-hearted and enthusiastic. He learnt that the project was progressing well with a carefully recruited team who worked well together. Jones felt a growing excitement and giving Craig and a couple of others a lift, drove the short distance to Brathay.

He came back down to earth on arrival at the plant. An untidy shambles of buildings in varying stages of construction set in a sea of muddy ruts, noisy with heavy machinery rumbling through. His workplace was a Nissan hut, already airless and with its corrugated iron curves, threatening to be stifling by midday. Outside a spluttering generator created enough electricity for a single overhead light and a lamp over a wooden desk. He could find nowhere to plug in an electric fan, supposing he could find one in the wilds of Cumberland. The one, narrow window above his desk was filthy with dust and mud from the building works and dead flies. He searched for something to clean it but had to resort to his handkerchief.

This proved to be a big mistake. Through the one small circle of smeared glass Jones had cleared, he caught sight of his only view … that damned field with the old standing stones. He sat back onto his swivel chair, curiously shaken up yet also feeling foolish. The young scientist spent the rest of his day being shown around the project by the management team and spending time organising his existing paperwork. Earlier that morning, he was shown the eventual site of the control rooms where he would be permanently based and this gave him a sense of hope and relief, they were not in sight of the curiously baleful Ryecroft Stones. For the rest of the day, Jones concentrated on his research notes, leaving the door of the hut wide open, even with the noise and dust from the construction. But despite the heat and oppressive humidity, he left the rest of the window uncleaned and closed shut. It would remain like that until the control rooms were ready and he could relocate from this miserable hut with the ominous view.

Eskscale had never been so busy since the war ended. There was much to welcome. The offcomers had brought many new jobs for the locals and the new families renewed life to the remote area. The school had to be enlarged to house more children and more teachers hired. Rev Winters preached to a packed church and began to hold more services to accommodate his new parishioners. There was understandable fear and shock at the power plant's vast size, dwarfing the cleared site of the old munition plant on which it now stood. The strangeness of its out of place, science fiction design wore off too and gradually became an accepted part of the scenery. Yet the unease felt by many over its proximity to the Stones remained like a bitter aftertaste to those who feared them. Constant reassurance from the government officials behind the plant, helped allay fears of the atomic power being created so close to their homes. It was going to create safe, clean energy, something to be proud of.

The increasingly outnumbered old Eskscale families did what they could to lessen the danger from Ryecroft field itself. They got together and built a wooden fence topped with barbed wire to surround the field. A strongly worded letter from the land's absentee landowner's solicitor demanded the fence be removed. The locals ignored it, in a battle of determination and increasingly angry correspondence that stretched out for a year.

Flora and her children's life would have been blissful and contented but for that wretched field. An anxiety they shared that never left their minds for long. Life married to Jed was more than she could have ever dreamt of. She had never known such overwhelming love for a man before. Her late husband had been a good man in the short time they had together before the war took him from her life forever. Jed brought out a passionate side to Flora, something she had never experienced before. To make her happiness complete, Rowan and Ash adored him. Indeed, Ash had all the makings of a future farmer, avidly learning from Jed, and becoming a huge help to him at lambing time. Yet, Flora could never shake off a sense that this contentment was on borrowed time. Nor did she ever forget that Freddie Adams should have been with them. Should have been family.

The furtive shadows were still seen occasionally among the Stones, though the locals now chose not to mention them at all. The boom in prosperity would not cease because of the sightings, but no one wanted to look a superstitious fool in front of the offcomers.

Then came the 'incident'.

The obduracy of his superiors infuriated Rhys Jones: top scientists who were answerable to damn pen pushers. Bureaucrats based in London, including many who had served as officers during the war and expected those on a lower pay scale to jump to their command. Jones, despite his youth was a highly accomplished scientist and found this outdated attitude bordering on insane. What Jones and the team were working on was pioneering, world changing but far more dangerous than the pen pushers wanted to hear. Nor did the general public know this plant was not just for producing electricity but also weapons' grade plutonium. In the rush to get Brathay completed, short cuts were taken. Contaminated waste was pumped straight into the Irish Sea and large amounts of radioactive contaminated material were kept underwater in open, outdoor pools. In Jones' opinion, this cavalier attitude could not end well.

He was not at work the night the alarms went off: the shrieking banshee wails everyone hoped never to hear. It was a short-lived warning. Officials at the plant had told the local constabulary to calm down the locals, there had been a minor accident at Brathay but there was no danger to the region. Jones drove to the plant but was refused entry at the gates. All the staff were given leave and records of what happened suppressed. It took some time for some details to emerge. Three technicians, men that Jones had worked with, had been killed outright in a small but lethal explosion. A local man had received radioactive burns to his face and chest. Once allowed back to work, Jones found nothing had changed. The headlong rush to complete the plant continued and it was considered bad form to comment on the deaths. Nothing so pioneering came without a cost, was the official view. Jones vowed never to forget the men who had died, even though it was forbidden for plant staff to contact their families.

Henry Jaggard, GordonTerry and Frank Bainsbridge. He would remember their names and honour their sacrifice to progress, if no one else did.

Within days of the first funeral of the accident victims, Rhys Jones began to have nightmares. Ones so vivid, they did not fade to nothing during the morning. Blurred, dark, shadowy images, a cacophony of unearthly whispers. Faint, angry words that made no sense, nor could humans replicate such malign, eldritch sounds. A man of science and logic, yet he was in no doubt he was being haunted by something supernatural. Something trying to communicate with him with considerable urgency. Jones had no doubt it was connected to the nuclear plant and the Drwg Stones. His ancient, cultural heritage lay deep in his bones, he was descended directly by the first people to inhabit these isles when the Great Ice finally relinquished its glacial grip. The same people who built enigmatic stone circles across the country and in North France, also a home of his Brythonic ancestors. At first, he thought his fear of the Ryecroft circle was unfounded, totally ridiculous. Jones now sensed he must stop relying on his Twentieth Century logic and dig deeper into the past. These Stones were different, they were wrong and he needed to know why.

Since he had moved to Eskscale, the locals had been friendly and welcoming but closed down instantly when anyone mentioned Ryecroft Field. They dismissed it as something old and unimportant but as a careful observer of body language, he could not help noticing the shake of hands holding beer tankards, the unwillingness to maintain eye contact.

From his Fellside home, the man stumbled outside as if the sharp night air would disperse the angry, alien clamour tormenting him. He could not understand their speech, sibilant and painful to his ears and brain. Every encounter in the past had made his ears and eyes bleed, gave him headaches lasting for days that no medication could ease. The voices had left him alone for three years, now they were back and their fury close to intolerable. There was nothing he could do to prevent their attacks on him. The only choice was to obey. He had to go back to the Stones. Something had enraged the Drood and there was only one way to satiate them, yet another blood sacrifice.

The realisation that he was being used, was no more than a puppet of living flesh and bone had hit hard as he tried to renew his old life back in London. He had believed he was immune so far away from Cumberland to the strident clamour torturing his mind. A letter from some London law firm had changed all that. Out of curiosity, he had visited the firm and discovered from them that he was now a wealthy man, one with considerable property. Once more he had felt the yoke of servitude tighten across his narrow shoulders. The property was near Eskscale and the fortune that came with it, would only be his if he lived there at an old family home permanently. He could not run from this fate; the shadows would follow and torment him wherever he lived.

So, haunted and in permanent distress, he had returned to the wretched Fells. To a large crumbling mansion, bleak in outlook and interior. He ignored the decrepit state of the place and extensive grounds. What was the point in restoring it when it was merely a lair, somewhere to hide waiting his instructions from his eldritch masters. He could not bear to see his appearance, knowing his face looked crazed, haggard, his hair and beard long and unkempt. He covered all the reflective surfaces, knowing the sight of what he had become would tip him even deeper into madness. He had arranged for prepaid deliveries of food and any mail to be left by the kitchen door. He survived but not thrived despite his new fortune as a recluse, unknown and unseen. His tormentors would not allow him to live in any other way.

They wanted the earth soaked in human blood and he must give it to them. Only that would calm their invasion of his mind, a most likely bring brief respite from the screeching demands in a language he did not understand yet the chilling meaning was all too clear.

9

Calling out, Ash rushed into the farmhouse, scattering the cats slumbering by the Aga and setting all the dogs into a barking frenzy. Jed wasn't at home but he found his mother and sister in the parlour, studying some old herbal books.

'Mam! There's a gang of offcomers,' he gasped, fighting for breath, 'getting ready to tear down the fence around Ryecroft field.'

Flora gave a slight sigh, 'It was to be expected, we've had a whole year without the owner acting over the fence.'

'But Mum, those men may go into the field,' Ash insisted, 'remember the day when it was crawling with tourists and the ground beneath them moved.'

Unlike most of the Eskscale inhabitants at the time, Flora did not choose to forget, though she had joined their closed ranks with them and remained silent. Any wild talk of earthquakes and possible subsidence would have delayed or scupper plans for the power plant. A development that meant so much for the future prosperity of the area. What happened that day did sharpen her focus on the Drood, or perhaps more accurately spelt, the Drwg. The evil ones. Someone had to.

'Could have done without all this.'

The foreman of the men hired to remove the wall,

pushed back his flat tweed cap and scratched his bald head.

'Bloody sheep shaggers.'

The team were all from a firm based in the city of Lancaster, outsiders to this crowd of Cumberland yokels who had gathered in a hostile silence along the road. The team had been extremely well paid by their hirer, some money already in their pockets, the rest on completion of the task. They had been warned the locals would object to the removal of the fence and had come prepared with knuckle dusters and coshes hidden in their clothes. No sign of the law either, the team would not start a ruckus with this lot, but they were determined to finish one. Such good money just to legally pull down a fence was not to be easily lost.

The ominous silence from the watching local broke into enthusiastic murmurs. They moved aside to allow a tall woman to pass through and approach the outcomer team. Their foreman walked towards her, hoping she was a sign of no hostility. The law was on their side after all. Her expression was solemn but she held out her hand in polite greeting which the foreman shook.

'Flora Barrows, the people of Eskscale have asked me to speak for them.'

'Jim Evans, I lead this work team hired by the field's owners to remove this illegal fence.'

The woman gave a slight smile and sighed, her voice calm and strong.

'I understand you have your work to do, Mr Evans but this fence is highly important to us. The field is dangerous. Many people have been injured amongst the Stones, some badly. We even had a brutal murder in here too, not that long ago. You gentlemen can leave and return to your safe homes. We have to live with this danger, the fence is important to protect visitors and newcomers moving to Eskscale.'

The woman's argument sounded reasonable. Evans had been warned these people were backward, superstitious. There was none of the expected talk of demons, if the field was dangerous for everyday physical reasons, keeping it fenced off seemed perfectly reasonable. There was already warning signs up along the perimeter, there must be room for a peaceful compromise. He put this solution to the woman.

'Such signs seem to be a challenge to some young folk,' she said, glancing across the field and shuddering, 'ignoring them a sign of youthful rebellion. We need something more substantial, a physical barrier. Whoever owns Ryecroft field, they are not locals and have never made themselves known to us. How could they possibly understand?'

Again, everything the woman said made sense, but Evans had a job to do, his men were expecting a good financial reward. Especially after making the long drive from Lancaster at an unearthly hour that morning, it took them three hours along the winding and often rough roads.

'I am sorry, miss,' Evans said, scratching his scalp under his cap again, 'we've been hired to do a legitimate job. I understand your concerns but we have no choice.'

Flora stepped back and shrugged.

'I am sorry too, Mr Evans. We have no choice either.'

She walked back to the waiting villagers, all long-time Eskscale folk but this time joined by a crowd of curious offcomers, the new villagers. They were not there to protest, just wondering what was going on but their arrival greatly outnumbered the workmen. The atmosphere became more charged, more confrontational.

Evans called his team over, out of earshot of the locals.

'No one is going to lose out on their wages. But I'm not going to get you into a scrap with these yokels. It's not a big job. Any volunteers to come back with me at three am, when all the buggers will be fast asleep? We can get it done quickly with no trouble.'

'Overtime?'

'After it is done, yeah, why not.'

Three of the men agreed and the work team got back in their cars and vans and drove away, seething at the cheers of the village idiots. Let the fools celebrate, mused Evans. His Lancastrian Lads would have the last laugh, in his mind. They always did.

'I reckon those *gadgees* will be back, after dark.'

Jed Barrows took another sip of whiskey and looked up at his wife as she pushed aside the dogs and sat beside him on their well-worn but comfortable sofa.

'Most likely,' she agreed, nursing her own drink, intended to steady her nerves but failing, 'but what else could I say to the foreman. I made our concerns over the field's safety to sound understandable and totally reasonable.'

Jed nodded. He agreed but it wouldn't diminish the peril those men faced if they returned after dark. They also had every legal right to be on the land, day or night. There was nothing Sergeant Brodie could do beyond arresting anyone from Eskscale for interfering. Something was stirring up the Drood shadows though. After relatively quiet years, their furtive, eerie shades were seen by many passing Ryecroft field, and by an increasing number of offcomers. The old family locals tried to give a natural reason for the sightings to stop any fear mongering. They were desperate to stop anything that would put off visitors or offcomers bringing jobs and prosperity to Eskscale. Some had come to Flora, imploring her to use some spell or ritual to banish the Drood. This had saddened and frustrated her. If only she could, the creatures' haunting would have been stopped long ago.

Flora watched as her husband finished his whiskey. This was the first and hopefully last time she had used her herbal skills on him. She had slipped a tasteless sleeping draught into his drink, one that would send him into a deep, restful slumber. A man as hard working as Jed often fell asleep on the sofa in front of a fire crackling in the hearth. There was no need for him to suspect anything surreptitious. Flora did not want this good man harmed by the Drood or a gang of angry workmen. With the children sound asleep upstairs, she prepared to leave the house. She had no plan, no idea what she was going to do. She was as vulnerable as any other person to whoever, whatever had been shedding blood among the Stones. There was no doubt the creatures had first grown stronger after the murder of Mrs Smythe and when that unfortunate tourist had severed an artery, spraying blood like a fountain over the field and Stones. Had that unfortunate hiker from London also been a victim? He had been found totally exsanguinated.

'You cannot go back there by yourself.'

Rowan, fully dressed, came down the stairs. Flora started to say something but was reminded by the girl's determined posture that her daughter was no longer a child but a young woman on the edge of sixteen. One who had begun her training as a witch in her thirteenth year on her first visit of the moon. She had inherited her father's raven black hair and Flora's golden-brown eyes and willpower. Flora's own eyes welled with tears of love and pride; Rowan was already a formidable young woman.

'And I cannot risk your precious life, my darling lass.'

'We have to do something, mam. Neither of us could bear another innocent life lost in that damned field.'

There was no point trying to argue with her daughter, Flora nodded and held the door open to her. They walked out into a night eerily silent, their route to the Stones overlooked by a canopy of coldly indifferent stars.

He was alone, fuming that the other workers had not turned up to help him. Jim Evans parked his van on the layby beside the field and turned off the headlights. He waited in the van for some time, looking for any lights or movement that could be locals guarding the site. The darkness around him was intense, something he had never experienced in the city. With no moon, the landscape was silent, shrouded and hostile, without him knowing why. An inner voice told him to go back. Another, more strident and stubborn insisted he get on with job. He reached over, grabbed his bag of tools and got out of the van. Nobody was there, no lurking yokels. The countryside was slumbering, as he should he, back with his ol'lass in Lancaster. He laughed at his own idiocy and taking a torch and a big wire cutter out of the bag, began to take down the offending fence.

Glad of the extra thick work gloves, Evans made good progress with the wire, strung alone on top of the wooden stakes in a continuous jagged roll. He'd hooked himself a few times by steel barbs ripping above the gloves but his heavy wool pea jacket protected him well. He paused, taking stock at what he had already achieved. One whole section of the wire was torn down from the front of the field. If he worked hard, Evans believed he could have the whole lot gone within a couple of hours. Plenty of time to take a sledge hammer to the wooden stakes, after all, it didn't have to be a neat job. He pushed on, ignoring the suggestion of shadowy, silent shapes gathering in the field by the old stones, tricks caused from the lack of light and his imagination. That was caused by that damned local woman putting stupid ideas into his head, this was just a scruffy field. No danger at all.

Damn. He had dropped the heavy cutters while reaching up to the wire with tiring arms. They had landed on the other side of the stone wall, in the field. He shone his torch down to find them but they were instantly hidden by the tufts of tangled brambles and nettles hugging the stone wall. The wire cutters were an expensive tool, bought brand new for this job. Evans stood back, his mind in disarray. He could easily climb over the field gate and retrieve them. Yet part of his thoughts yelled, get into the van and go home. Forget the cutters, forget the job. Get back to the wife and young uns.

Anger built up within him. Centred at the weakening power of suggestion planted in his mind by that red headed woman. Jim Evans had fought with courage and distinction in the war, he'd survived the D Day landings and helped push the Nazis across Europe all the way to the ruins of Berlin. There was nothing he couldn't handle in an empty field in the dark. The largest predatory wild animals in this country were lithe, small foxes and stocky badgers, none a danger to a human. In war-torn

Europe, he'd camped in snow bound, deep woods complete with winter starved wolves and bears. He walked back to the field gate, now free of wire and clambered over.

Shining the torch downwards, he walked back to where he had dropped the cutters. A sound made him pause, a car approaching but still some distance away. He crouched down behind the wall, feeling foolish. He was not doing anything wrong; he had the legal right to be in the field, regardless of the time of day. Yet an old forgotten memory resurfaced, a story in a newspaper years ago that had got so many tongues wagging, the horrific murder of a widow in a Cumberland village. Eskscale ... this field was the murder scene ... an unsolved crime. Evans had gone too far to turn back on such an idiotic fear, yet he kept his head down as he neared the spot where the cutters had landed. They'd make a useful weapon ... more mad thoughts. There was no more sound of a car engine, must have just been someone returning home late.

He pulled off a long, study branch of hazel and began to brush aside the undergrowth, trying to find the metallic gleam of the lost tool. The torch beam flickered as if about to fail. Again, Evans swore, cussing his decision to come back in the dark. As he shook the torch as if to fix a loose connection, the flickering light revealed a surrounding vision of horrors. Monstrous black bodies, taller than humans, thin and sinuous as snakes. No features, just blazing orbs in place of eyes. One shadow was different, black, featureless but human in form. It held something, the torch in his wavering hand catching the gleam of metal ... his wire cutters! Evans shrieked, fell forward as he tried to escape only to be impaled on something broad, blunt that drove upwards, underneath his sternum and crushed his heart. He was dead before he fell, his body entangled in the twisted roll of barbed wire.

The women did their best to rush along the road to the Stones without using their torches. Confronting a gang of men in the darkness was madness, Flora and Rowan had no plan, just an overwhelming need to prevent loss of life by any means they could. As their eyes became adjusted to the darkness, familiarity with the road helped them hurry. Rowan paused and held up her hand for her mother to do the same. A car on the move away from them, tyres screeching as it rounded corners at speed. They paused in case the vehicle turned around and headed back to Eskscale but it continued its engine revving flight, heading toward the Fells until they could no longer hear it.

They pushed on with greater urgency, maybe the car leaving was a good sign that the workers had gone away unharmed. On arrival at the field, Flora's premonition of badness returned. She could see the foreman's van parked by the wall, its headlights acting as a light source. Much of the barbed wire and some of the fencing had already been demolished. She risked making herself known,

'Mr Evans! Jim? It's Flora Barrows ... I just want to make sure you are alright.'

Silence. Not even the scuffle or flutter of disturbed night creatures. Such deep silence was uncanny and unnatural. They shone their torches across the field and saw nothing untoward, no furtive shadows but no workmen either. Something gleamed as Flora's torch passed over the field's edge, close to the wall. At first she could not make sense of the crumpled form. She moved closer, making out awkwardly sprawled limbs tangled in barbed wire. She bit deeply into her clenched fist to stifle a horrified gasp. Jim Evans' body was slumped forward, propped up by a large metal tool plunged deep into his chest. With his head dropped down, she was spared the agonised expression on the victim's face

'Get back, darling,' Flora urged, wanting to spare her daughter from the grisly sight. There was nothing they could do for the poor man. It was better that they were not found at a murder scene. There would be enough awkward questions once the police were involved. Perhaps The Stones had claimed another life but Flora believed this killing was not caused by any supernatural act. This was a violent murder by a living human, she remembered hearing that car speeding away. She grabbed Rowen's hand and pulled her away from the field.

'We must hurry home. We were not here tonight. Do you understand? We never left the house.'

The inevitable furore descended on the village in a chilling echo of the past murders. The same big presence of police interrogating the locals, the same irritating swarm of newspaper reporters fishing for a grisly story to titillate their ghoulish readership. Once again a pall of shock and dread enveloped the village causing shudders of fear among those who believed the Stones were cursed.

At the inquest, there was no forensic evidence of anybody else at the scene of Evan's gruesome demise. The verdict was an accidental death, one of those freak ones that make the news and become nothing more than a strange anecdote to all but the victim's grieving family and close friends. Jim Evans had been a popular man by all accounts and the inquest court had been packed. Once again, Flora held her tongue. Had she spoken, the world beyond Eskscale would have dismissed her as an attention seeking lunatic. What good would that do? How would that help Evans' widow come to terms with her loss?

Her belief that the man was murdered by an all too human maniac, perhaps under the control of the Drood, destroyed any lingering peace of mind. Flora had never been more afraid. One thing that helped her endure the tragedy was Rowen's complete acceptance of her mother's plea for silence. In this modern century as in so many others where strict adherence to organised religion held sway, silence was the only way for a witch to stay safe, a centuries old conspiracy of protective silence. But matters at Eskscale were escalating, more and more Drood sightings, still only within the circle of stones. If they gained enough power and malign intent to go beyond Ryecroft field, Flora would break the silence to protect her family and the community. That was why she was here, her destiny and now she was no longer alone, she had Rowan at her side.

Her greatest fear now was not just the shadows, maybe it was a mortal who did their bidding, who had taken at least three lives to serve them. It could be anyone, someone she already knew and trusted. It may even be more than one assailant, whoever killed them must have had a manic strength. Flora wondered if she would ever be able to sleep in peace and contentment again.

10

Eskscale, September 1954

Whoever, whatever was placating the evil in Ryecroft field had become crafty, of this, Flora was certain. Curiously, blood soaked so quickly into the stony soil there, it left no visible trace but there had been no murders or unfortunate 'accidents' for five years. That did not mean the killings hadn't happened elsewhere and the victim's blood brought to the Stones. She paused from her work, the kitchen table in front of her covered in freshly picked wild and cultivated plants and tree bark ready to make tinctures and potions. She sensed deep in her bones that a dank, cold winter was to come and wanted to be ready to help the villagers with their ailments. There was no village doctor at that time, not since dear old Doctor Lucas had passed. Never retiring, the man was still caring for his patients in his late eighties. There was never any rivalry between the two healers. Flora would insist people saw their village GP if needed and he would recommend her tinctures and mixtures over some conventional medicines. It seemed no offcomer medic wanted to set up in the village preferring bigger, more lively towns like Whitehaven. Flora couldn't blame them.

She had more patients to take care of now, with the many offcomers settling in to Eskscale life, blissfully unaware of the danger so close to the village. An unknown threat that was not the obvious hazard from

Brathay's vast brutish towers at the atomic power station. That was a tangible reminder of very real peril to the locals and far beyond. What was once welcomed for bringing work and wealth to this remote, wind-blown region, was now regarded as a necessary evil. A view reinforced by the grievous loss of the three local men and the maiming of another in an accident. Men sacrificed to the relentless altar of progress and a promised gleaming future of peace and prosperity. To add to this mental turmoil, Flora could not allay her anxiety from whatever haunted Ryecroft field, both supernatural and all too human.

'Hi mam, need a hand?'

Flora shook off her melancholic thoughts as Rowan walked in, her legs hidden by a happy, welcoming whirl of the farm's dogs and cats. Both the Barrow's children now commuted by the coastal train to Whitehaven for their secondary education. So lost in her work and anxious musing, Flora had forgotten the time. She didn't need to ask where Ash was, his first thoughts on arriving home was always the farm livestock and being in Jed's company. Rowan had her mind set on university and a career in medicine, Ash had the heart and soul of a hill farmer and would never willingly leave the Fells. He'd even picked up Jed's broad Cumbrian accent and dialect words. Ash was a Barrows now, in name and deed, his awareness of his actual father remained a black and white photo on the mantelpiece and his mother's tears when memories inevitably emerged. Flora smiled at her daughter.

'I'm getting addlepated, too preoccupied to note the time. Can you put this stuff away for me, *hinny*, I will get the tea ready.'

This afternoon, instead of pulling on overalls over his

school uniform and tending to his own livestock, Ash ran straight to the farmhouse to find his mother.

'Ash? What about riding up to check on your Herdwick weanlings. BonBon could do with the exercise. You spoil that Fell. She was bred to be a working animal not a show pony.'

'The wedders will be fine, Ma. I will go after I tell you summat.'

Nothing stood in the way of caring for his animals, Flora knew her son had something important to say. She left off peeling potatoes on the kitchen worktop and gestured for him to sit down at the table with Rowan.

'One of the younger lasses at my school, wee Katie Lesh was in a right aald state, well flaiten. She swore by Sweet Baby Jesus that she had seen black, oily shadows from her bedroom window. Two were creeping along the lane up by the Kesh farm last night. Long and thin shadows with no faces.'

Flora's mind raced with confusion. If this was true, the Drood men were now able to leave the Ryecroft field boundary but for what reason? And why now after being contained there for millennia. She was still convinced a madman had done the killings for some ghastly ritual. Were these things more than just eerie shadows? Could they kill too?

'Who did she tell?'

'Her teacher, Mrs Worth and in front of the whole class. All the Whitehaven bairdens were laughing and mocking her. Calling her a divvy.'

'And Mrs Worth?'

'Told her off for making up silly stories.'

The Kesh family were from one of the oldest Eskscale dynasties, the name known from when the first records began and believed they were here even further back, when the land belonged to the Celtic people of the region, once their kingdom of Rheged. The child's father did not attend any of the recent informal meetings of the old families since the Drwg Stones crisis had begun. Maybe this might change when he saw his daughter's distress.

'Ash, I think the pony may get some exercise after all. You are right, the weanlings can wait. Could you wheel out the trap and get BonBon harnessed. I need to go out. You kids are old enough to get your own tea.'

Rowan rolled her eyes in mock exasperation.

'We've been telling you that for ages, Ma ...'

Though her meeting with Simeon Kesh, another hill farmer, would be awkward, Flora found herself enjoying driving the sturdy black pony, even along the busier lanes. For a short while, the beauty of her surroundings with the coast and grey sea to her left and the Fells to her right. The morning's cold, squally storm had past, leaving the autumn air cool, the remaining tawny foliage glossy with raindrops. Above the landscape, a rainbow shone against the retreating black storm clouds. The new offcomer residents and ever-growing number of tourists had brought more cars and buses, the power plant had brought more heavy lorries onto narrow, winding country roads. The valiant BonBon ignored the traffic with a stalwart resolve, even when idiots blasted their horns and drove too close. Flora relaxed more when she had crossed the village ... maybe small town was now more accurate, and turned the pony's head back up the Fells along a dirt track, mercifully mud and deep rut free. BonBon was brave, strong and active as befit an ancient native breed that dated back to Cumbria's

Brythonic days. They were once bred to be warhorses, usually born jet black, and had carried ancient Rheged's fierce fighters into battle.

Travelling to the Kesh farm, she was able to keep her back to dour and overwhelming presence of Brathay and the cursed field beside it. Living at Jed's farm instead of in the village had also been an enormous source of relief. The emanations from the Stones had increased dramatically since the construction of Brathay to the verge of being unbearable. The family were away from being too close in vicinity, at least for now. If little Katie was right, nowhere could be safe.

Unusually, the gate to the Kesh farm was firmly shut as Flora turned the pony down the track to the farm. A keep out sign was attached to it, a rare thing among the tight knit but hospitable Eskscale farming community. As she paused, looking for a safe place to tie BonBon up to allow her to try to open the gate, one of the Kesh lads approached, shotgun tucked under his arm. His face, drawn into an anxious scowl relaxed when he saw who had arrived. His welcoming smile was brief, strained but genuine.

'Thank you, Mrs Barrows, t'oll lass will be made up to see you.'

He released the padlock chaining the gate shut, opened it wide enough for the trap to get through and redid the lock on the gate. The Kesh family were afraid and there was no other obvious cause beyond what the child had seen. Johnny, the youngest of the five strapping Kesh sons remained behind as Flora urged the pony to trot down the long track to the farm. Perhaps the other boys were also on guard around the homestead. Their obvious unease made her mission easier, but still not one she looked forward to. Some instinct warned her that this was proof of the start of some grim, deadly days for the community. Whatever had begun with the grisly death of Mrs Smythe was escalating.

The farm yard itself was silent, as if under siege, BonBon's iron shod hooves clattering on the concrete, cartwheels whirring. No familiar dash of farm dogs ready to welcome or threaten the newcomer on their territory. No scurry and clutter of startled chickens … all the household livestock was shut away as were the family and farm workers. No familiar welcome from Ma Kesh, the matriarch of the Kesh clan, a formidable, robust woman even at ninety and a regular customer for Flora's herbal tonics, something the old lady swore by. Flora saw a kitchen curtain twitch and the main door of the house open with a gradual wariness.

'It's only me, Flora Barrows on my own.'

She heard a swift exchange of female voices; one, young, tremulous, the other the unmistakable strident tones of Ma Kesh. The door swung open and the older woman pushed aside a shotgun wielding teenage girl. Katie's older sister Nancy.

'Tek t'pony into t'barn with t'other beasts, Flora, keep it locked. Best to be safe.'

Flora nodded, no one argued against Violet Kesh in her own yard. With a content BonBon tethered inside the barn with a big net of sweet, summer cut hay, she returned across the empty barnyard. The yard was always kept immaculate but the lack of chickens, farm cats and dogs was chilling. Flora stepped inside the also spotless kitchen, the beating heart of the Kesh family, even for those living now across Cumbria in their own farmsteads. Violet held them here, united in her formidable embrace, a rare matriarch in a resolutely patriarchal society. A throwback perhaps to Rheged's female warriors or the fierce shield maidens of the later Norse settlers in the region. Flora was beckoned over to an old, overstuffed arm chair by an open fire with Violet settling in its twin opposite her. Three of the farm cats jumped onto the arm of Flora's chair, all purring and wanting to be petted. The old woman made no attempt to shoo them away, the cats knew her visitor was too special, too important to not to show their own form of feline respect.

'You're here to speak to our Katie.'

It was a statement of fact, not a question or a challenge.'

'Only if she wants to speak to me, Mrs Kesh. The poor child has been through so much. First seeing those things, the second being not believed and laughed at.'

'Not by us, her family, t'only ones that matter round these parts.'

Smiling, Flora accepted a mug of tea from Nancy, the girl's hands shaking with an uncharacteristic nervousness. Not of her visitor, Flora decided but fear of what she had come to talk about with Nancy's great grandmother. As if in answer, Nancy scurried away from the kitchen on some chore that had somehow suddenly become urgent. Violet made no comment on the girl's departure, it was not an act of inhospitality to their guest. Not today.

'The Drood Men are on the rise,' Violet continued, 'gan beyond their field. Nothing but evil will come to us now. Unless you can stop them. It's your destiny.'

Flora was dreading this. She had been given no guidance from her forebears, no ancestral wisdom handed down over centuries, beyond Ryecroft field was a bad place that must be left undisturbed. How could they have known about the massive changes wrought by the 20th century? What answer could she give? That she could only fail the community that trusted her?

'I was told no more than that the field was cursed by something from a time so distant it was long before any written records. How would my mother and grandmother know anything else? They only knew a time when the Stones were buried deep beneath the soil.'

Violet nodded, her face visibly blanching.

'Aye, we have only been handed down the last fading whispers of a spoken history of that field. Nowt much to go on, is it?'

There was a light, tentative tap on the kitchen door and it opened a couple of inches. They heard Nancy's voice attempting to scold a small child in a low whisper. The women could hear every word.

'Oh, let the bairden in,' Violet called out, 'it will do her good to talk to someone who will believe her.'

The older girl walked in with little Katie clinging onto her hand. The child's complexion was usually sun-kissed with a smattering of freckles across her nose and cheeks after a summer running free with her friends, the children too young to be much use on the farms. Now Katie was ashen, pale blue eyes wide and brimming with fresh tears. Flora held out her arms to her and the child broke free of her older sister and ran into their visitor's embrace. Flora held her tightly, letting the little girl release her emotions in a surge of heartrending sobbing. Stroking her hair, Flora waited until she finished crying. Raised to be tough and stoical, resilient to all the bad fortune a life in the Fells could deliver, what Katie had witnessed and her truth dismissed and ridiculed was beyond day to day life. The stern matriarch of the Kesh clan may not approve of mollycoddling a child but Flora knew this little one needed a good hug. Katie began to speak between gulps and sniffles, wiping away tears with the back of her hand.

'Mrs Barrows, ah wuz gay flaiten.'

'I know, Katie dear, and I totally believe you.'

This prompted more tears, this time of gratitude. Flora was patient and waited for the child to be ready to speak again.

'They wuz like smoke at first, pouring through our big farm gate. But then they wuz not smoke ... tall and skinny with oily, black bodies. And long claws like a cat's but much longer.'

She looked up at Flora, her eyes once more brimming with tears, 'they had no faces!'

'Why is this happening?'

Violet's voice betrayed anger beyond the dread.

'The Drood have been just an aald legend for as long as anyone could remember. Any sightings have been just shadows in that accursed field. Explainable ones, easy t'write off as an overactive imagination or a pint too many of strong ale. Now we have unexplained deaths and them monsters openly crossing beyond the walls around Ryecroft.'

With the child comforted from being believed, Flora had all she needed to arrange an urgent meeting with the old Eskscale families. Her suspicion that a human had done the ritualistic killings in and around Ryecroft field remained, what these unearthly things were capable of was a chilling unknown.

'I need to get back to Eskscale, Mrs Kesh, to try to warn the old families and as many of the new ones as possible.'

'Nancy, fetch Mrs Barrows' pony t'front of farm.'

Violet stood up and shook her head, recognising the

impossible task the village witch faced.

'Best of luck with that, hinny. They'll tek some convincing.'

Flora thanked the old lady for her hospitality and waited for the older girl to lead BonBon over to her.

'Old Ma Blamire still alive?'

Mrs Kesh muttered as her guest stepped up to the seat of the trap.

'Don't want to be last of my generation left in Eskscale.'

Smiling, Flora nodded.

'Plenty of your tough aald marras left. There's Ma Blamire, old Mr Salkeld and the Liddle sisters, all ninety plus and hale and hearty to my knowledge. Outlive us all, I reckon.'

'Reckon we will, if the Drood Men don't tek us.'

Flora gathered up the pony's reins but before moving off, she turned back to the Kesh matriarch.

'They will probably protest, loudly, menfolk being what they are, but all your family should be back in their homes behind locked doors come nightfall. We don't know what these things are capable of. Bullets might pass straight through them.'

Violet nodded assurance and Flora urged the pony into a brisk trot. At least the old woman's clan might be safer now; none of them would disobey the formidable Ma Kesh. Flora's family too, Jed would not need convincing. There was no such reassurance among the other old Eskscale families and none from the offcomer settlers. Why would they believe such a bizarre tale? How could she blame them? Had Flora been born and raised anywhere else, she would have thought such tales were too bizarre to be true.

Flora did not go straight home, too agitated by her

visit to the Kesh family to delay gathering the old Eskscale families under one roof. The Herdwick Tup had always hosted local meetings, every varied gathering from the Farmers Wives Club to wedding receptions. None would be as important and difficult as the one she was desperate to make happen. As Bon Bon's hooves clattered once back on the tarmac road again, Flora was grateful for the pony's steadfast manner, ignoring the ignorant, angry drivers hooting their car horns and driving too close to the pony and trap.

'Offcomers,' Flora gave a dour mutter after she praised the pony's calm behaviour, 'they haven't got a clue how much damage a pony and trap could do to their precious cars if they caused her to spook.'

She pulled up at Harry and Glenda Vale's cottage home on the edge of Eskscale and told the couple of her need for an urgent meeting as her friend unharnessed Bon Bon and settled her in a spare stable. This allowed Flora to rush over to the cottage. His wife ushered her into the kitchen, she could see the anxiety in Flora's eyes and rightly guessed the reason. Talk of the little Kesh girl's terrifying encounter had already spread among the Eskscale old families.

'You'll be needing to make some calls, lass,' said Glenda, handing over the old-fashioned candlestick telephone, 'save us having to drive up and down fells.'

Flora took the phone with a nod and smile of gratitude, so typical of the Vales, no questions asked or the slightest reluctance shown to help. The smile widening as Glenda handed her a notebook.

'You'll be needing this too, hinny, even our beloved wise woman would be unable to remember all the phone numbers.'

Glenda pulled on her overcoat, 'while you do that,

I'll drive down to the Tup, help Maggie set up the meeting room.'

It was only a short distance from the Vale's home to the village, an easy walk for most people. But as they were an old Eskscale family, walking past Ryecroft Field was no longer an option. Even in her sturdy Austin Cambridge, Glenda put her foot down hard on the accelerator as she passed the wretched field and its grim stone sentinels, her gaze fixed firmly on the road ahead.

With Jed at her side, Flora was surprised at the large number of the old Eskscale families and the speed they had arrived. Maggie Graham had shut the Tup early to the vexation of some regulars and a couple of tourists passing through. In a surprisingly short time, the spacious back room was full and the mood of the gathering subdued but not surprised. Unlike her teacher, little Katie Kesh's frightening encounter was believed and she was not the only one to experience a sighting of the Drood beyond the Ryecroft field boundary. With one local after another describing what they had seen recently, even Eskscale's scoundrel Ed Thwaite broke his silence and added his own frightening encounter. For once his tale was believed. Last to arrive was the Kesh matriarch with three of her oldest sons at her side. In a spontaneous reaction, the gathering rose to their feet in respect to a family at the very heart and soul of the oldest local community.

'This cannot go beyond these four walls,' Ma Kesh announced once the gathering sat back down, and became silent, 'not now anyway. There are too many good folk, both locals and offcomers needing work from that nuclear plant. We need to find a way to defeat the Drood and send them back to whatever hell they came from ... but it must be done with just us in this room.'

Inevitably, the focus now switched to Flora, her heart sinking with the impossible weight of the gathering's expectation from their wise woman. She felt far from wise now, her mind racing, trying to find the right words to say. There was nothing written down in ancient times about the Drood, the old stories handed down verbally over the centuries had become too vague, any details lost to time.

Her voice wavering and apologetic, Flora stood up to address the hopeful crowd.

'Nellie Blamire told me it was my job to defeat the Drood but how to do this was not handed down along my family's time line. Neither my mother or grandmother ever spoke of them. All has changed since the Stones were dug up.'

She felt Jed's comforting presence beside her, felt his work hardened hand reach for hers.

'But I will do all in my ability to gather information, to speak to those knowledgeable in such ancient lore. If it can be done, I will give everything I can to rid the world of the Drood,' she paused, glanced across the gathering. 'But I will need your support, even if it means confronting danger from these evil spirits.'

Flora sat back down, the answering, uncomfortable silence told its own tale, that she might have to be alone in Eskscale's battle with the Drood.

11

Walking home from Eskscale village, nine-year-old Gary Anson battled another high wind straight off the sea; the full force of the gale drove an icy rain like a million-minute hammers. At the end of the school day an ominous darkness had built up along the horizon and reached the coast as a bad storm. Pulling up his anorak hood, Gary had no problem avoiding the sight of the four huge cooling towers of Brathay Nuclear Plant and the terror lurking in the fields below them. A fear he kept to himself though he knew many shared it.

With his head down, he made a slow but trouble-free journey and fell in through the front door, exhausted and wet through to a rapturous greeting from Rags, the family terrier. He found his father laying the kitchen table for supper. A man of few words, Anson smiled at his son and threw him a towel. An ordinary late September day in Cumbria.

They were coming …

Gary heard the tramp and scuff of many feet along the coastal path, still at some distance from his small cottage home. He wanted to see them, badly, curiosity stoked to fever pitch by schoolyard gossip. He waited, lingering over his supper of bread and warm dripping for a chance to unbolt the door and sneak outside, too anxious to speak in case he blurted out his intentions.

At last, his father arose from the kitchen table and

tucking a copy of the Daily Mirror under his arm, headed off to the garden outhouse, terrier trotting at his heels like a tan and white shadow. This bought Gary enough time, the boy opened the front door with all the stealth his nine-year-old self could muster and ran to the front gate, ignoring the spiteful squall still blowing in hard off the sea.

The protest march was already in sight, a large, straggling group of people coming through the seaside village of Eskscale and making their way, weary but determined to reach the four steaming cooling towers of Brathay that loomed above the valley like a medieval stronghold of monstrous size. They cast a long shadow, those towers, a symbol of a new, and to many, frightening power created elsewhere at the plant. One that could bring light and warmth to the homes of Great Britain or destroy the world in a curse of mushroom clouds and raining death.

Gary heard the rumours about the protest march the day before at school. Know all, Bert Thwaite had instructed the class that these people hated the new nuclear plant and had marched all the way from London to make their anger known. London - to the kids of a remote Cumberland village - seemed impossibly exotic and far away.

'Bloody daft buggars,' Thwaite had announced, delighted by their rapt attention, and echoing his father's exact words, risking a clip around the ear from a teacher if overheard for his swearing, 'walking all that way for pigging nowt. A load of dirty, bloody long hairs and good for nothing beatniks.'

Like Gary's dad had been, Thwaite senior was now employed at the nuclear works, as were so many from the Eskscale area. Brathay had put food on their tables and a roof over their heads after work from the old war time munitions factory had gone with its closure. Others, the boffins had moved there with their families. Scientists and engineers from all over the country came to live in and near the village and work at the plant. With all the benefits Brathay had brought, the new jobs were welcomed. The newcomers had become part of the wider community, though there was always an unspoken and mysterious barrier between them and the village locals.

This was why Gary doubted these protesters would get a warm welcome on the windswept coast lapped by the cold, wild Irish Sea. What idiots they must be, to choose to march past what could be a hostile populace. Young Bert Thwaite had hastily organised a plan for the village lads to hide along the route and pelt the marchers with beach pebbles and rotten eggs but like all his grandiose schemes, it had come to nothing. No one listened to a nine-year-old blowhard whose mother, feared as a mouthy battle axe was not to be messed with. When the march had tramped through the village, Gary was certain that a subdued Bert would be sitting in the kitchen having his bread and scrape tea like all the other kids.

Gary had grabbed his father's timely visit to the outhouse as an opportunity not to be missed, worth earning a right paddling afterwards. He stood, feet resting on a bar of the gate to get higher and watched the marchers pass by, many weighed down by heavy rucksacks and wielding Ban the Bomb placards. They were clearly soaking wet, foot sore and tired, the older ones of which there were many, dragging their feet, shoes scuffed and muddy. With the large cooling towers of the nuclear plant in sight, the younger ones broke into protest songs, accompanied by their battered acoustic guitars. Gary had never heard music like it but was not impressed, preferring the exciting new electric guitar twang on the radio, coming from America, like Bill Haley and the Comets or the new homegrown star Tommy Steele.

Occasionally someone from the march would turn and smile at the boy, or give a kindly wave or wink. They did not seem the crazy people of Bert's description just ordinary folk with some point to make. Guilty, Gary let the stone he'd grabbed from the front path drop from his hand. What was so wrong about the plant that made these people leave the comfort of their home to walk all this way, not even letting a storm stop their slow progress? He hated the plant because of the harm it had caused his family. But why did it bother these shuffling or striding protesters?

Rags rushed past his feet and began to berate the strangers with loud yaps and growls, the sight of the furious but very small dog leaping up and down with only her head showing above the fence like a jack in the box lightened the mood of the marchers, many laughed at her antics.

Gary heard his father approach, bellowing at Rags to shut up and the boy braced himself for a scolding but instead, he felt strong hands gently grip his shoulders and turn him towards their house. But not before Gary had seen the familiar looks from the marchers on seeing his father's face, first the inevitable shock, then revulsion and sometimes pity. An accident early on during construction had left Anson with terrible burns on his hands and face from scalding radioactive water.

'Rags ... I said whisht ... Now.'

Gary's father scooped up the still frantic terrier and

118

holding her tightly under his arm, returned down the path with his son.

'Come along, lad. You are soaking wet again, you daft apeth! You won't want your scran to go to waste.'

Back inside, Anson made a fresh pot of tea and sat in silence at the kitchen table as his son wolfed the last piece of bread. There was no anger in his manner towards his son's boyish curiosity or the marchers who wanted to do away with the town's most generous livelihood. Life had dealt him enough bad cards to get stressed now by what he could not change.

'Best stay away from cooling towers and t' Stones for a while, son, he advised, 'them marchers are likely to stir up trouble with the locals. T'army are already there protecting the perimeter fences.'

He took a swig of hot tea, 'As long as they say what they want, get it off their chests and go back home before the Queen arrives to open plant in October, I reckon this will be nowt but storm in a tea cup.'

Gary nodded. In truth he needed no persuading. The nuclear plant with its jumble of new brutish buildings and the huge, looming towers had always frightened him. There were the bad memories too, of the shrieking sirens that rent the night above Eskscale when his father had been maimed and three men killed by the explosion. Of his mother's screams of terror and grief and of the distress created by her refusal to accept what his father had become. How could he also forget her betrayal when she packed her bags and ran off late one night leaving her husband and young son behind? Yes. The plant had ruined their lives and Gary hated and feared it. When Gary left home for school, he kept his eyes focused on the village below, avoiding all sight of the towers. On the way home, he kept his eyes averted downwards, preferring to look at the path and his shoes rather than the four steaming monsters. In some strange way it was his attempt to block out the pain that the sight of the place caused him.

To add to his fear and misery, in a meadow below the nuclear plant was the circle of ten ancient stones, silent witnesses to a brash, frightening new age. Like all the long-term inhabitants from Eskscale, Gary knew why the Stones had been kept buried for so long.

To stop the rise of the Drood Men.

Yolanda Brown tucked a persistent lock of her greying brown hair back into her sodden woollen hat. A futile gesture, the biting, rain-lashed wind off the sea that scoured this flat, featureless landscape would free it again to whip her face, her eyes. This was the worst section of the long march despite nearing their destination. They were all weary, cold and soaking wet, finding it hard to keep up the spirit and morale that had fired them up since leaving London.

Nothing confirmed the righteousness of their cause more than the first sight of the nuclear power plant's towers. What exactly were these monuments to a dangerous new technology emitting? What was the nature of those constant trails of steam rising to poison the atmosphere? Only evil could come from there, the very substance, the toxic heart of nuclear bombs that could destroy the planet. That in a month's time, the place would be providing electricity to heat and light Cumberland homes was not enough to expedite the horror of nuclear power.

She had needed little persuading to go on the march. A single woman with no ties and a dead-end job in a library. She had read the arguments against Brathay and believed every word with a burning fervour that gave determination to every step on the march.

But now there was something else. As she approached Brathay, Yolanda felt a creeping sensation of extreme dread, a wrongness that owed nothing to the huge power plant but to something older, deeper and more inexplicable. At first she pushed it aside, the foolish notion of an ageing spinster in need of a hot bath and long rest. For all her determination to ignore it, the feeling refused to be ignored and became only stronger. She glanced at the faces of the others, searching for anyone with the same sense of alarm but there were none.

Yolanda began to hang back, getting farther away from the head of the march until they rounded a bend in the road and she could see an ancient stone circle. She froze, someone moved among them, a shadow? No - a tall, faceless thing made of shadow, black as pitch, thin and sinuous as a trail of smoke. The woman shrieked then fainted, immediately surrounded by concerned fellow marchers. As she came too, sitting slumped on the damp asphalt road, the trembling would not stop. She would not move another step closer to Brathay.

For the second time that afternoon, Rags the terrier went into a frantic, spinning excitement. She leapt at the door, alerting the Anson household they had unexpected visitors. Normally Gary rushed to answer, to spare his father the pain of strangers' reaction to his maiming but this time Anson was closer. A small group of protesters had gathered outside, supporting a woman who was in a state of shock, her face spectral pale, her whole body weak and shaking.

Anson needed no explanation. He nodded agreement to her helpers and he took the woman into his kitchen, set her down in the old armchair in front of the hot range. Gary watched as she took a mug of hot sweet tea from his father's damaged hands, she did not flinch away but managed a weak smile of gratitude. This woman was welcome in their home, the boy decided. Especially as it was obvious to him, she had seen one of them. He wanted the visitor to tell him what she saw, whether it was the same faceless creature with a body made of oily black smoke. But she was frail and exhausted. His father made her comfortable with a wool blanket over her thin shoulders and to no one's surprise, she fell into a deep slumber.

Gary was not taken aback his father let the woman stay awhile in their small, two up, two down home. No one with an ounce of kindness in their heart would let a frail stranger out in this weather, and his father had far more than an ounce of compassion. Anson had insisted she slept a while on their parlour couch, wrapped in wool blankets. She was in no state to walk back to Eskscale let alone start the long journey home to wherever she came from. Gary was delighted, for him, there had been no other reliable witness to the Drood Men. If adults had seen them, they kept quiet, at least in front of children. School kids' tales were unreliable and often downright idiotic. Like Bert Thwaite's frequently repeated boast of catching a Drood Man by its long red nose and spinning it around until it shrieked in surrender and bolted away.

Gary knew he was talking rubbish; he had seen one for himself.

12

Rhys Jones stood up and eased his aching back, painful from bending over the plant schematics for hours. Anxiety did not help his stressed muscles from scrutinising plans for disposal of low-level radioactive waste, his stress levels had gone through the roof. Some waste was already being pumped into the Irish Sea; this was not considered a problem, the radioactive levels too small to cause any damage. Other deposits were left underwater in deep open pools around the plant site.

It was the underground storage of the more dangerous waste that caused Jones sleepless nights. He was convinced the manufacture of the lead barrels it was pumped into, was deeply flawed, a rush job tendered out to the cheapest not the best. His superiors had batted aside his fears, the stuff was deep underground, what did it matter?

The water table was what mattered. Jones had argued with a futile passion and subsequently was on the brink of losing his job at Brathay. While he worked there, he was sworn to official secrecy because weapons grade plutonium was produced here. So in the interests of national security, they kept him on rather than letting him loose to become a nuisance, a whistle blower. The penalties for a plant employee who had signed the official secrets act breaking their contract, would be severe. It could even be considered treasonable, punishable by capital punishment. Silence or the hangman's noose.

Jones could not let go of his anxiety over the contamination. He began a secret journal, listing all the reckless decisions made at Brathay and who had made them. He hid the evidence under a floorboard at his digs in Whitehaven and prayed he would never have to use them.

Adding to his stress, he had been haunted by eerie voices at bedtime … faint at first but the continuing nightmares had worsened, the eerie voices becoming more strident, a loud clamour in his mind that began to spill-over into daytime. His colleagues began to notice his increasingly gaunt features, his occasional lapses of focus. His closest friends at Brathay, Gerard Craig and Jean Sherrington, rallied around, concerned at his appearance.

'Not the best of days, old chum,' Craig said at lunchtime, 'I think you could do with a break from this hot house of intense science. Grab a bite and a swift pint with me and Jean at the Tup.'

'Not the best day by a long chalk,' Jones replied, 'Not with all those protestors gathering outside our gates. I'm not risking riling the army lads either by gadding about beyond their protective cordon.'

Craig sighed and agreed.

'In that case, it's a good strong coffee with a drop or two of some smuggled in Scottish nerve bracer then … I'll bring one over.'

As the technician strolled away, the clamour began again in Jones' mind. The loudest yet. This wasn't a personal assault on him, he sensed. It was a warning.

Reaching the heavily fortified entrance to Brathay, the situation was more challenging than the protest leaders had expected. The presence of heavily armed soldiers around the entire perimeter was a shock, they had expected to see the local police but not this. Nor were they anticipating a wide ring of razor wire across the road in front of the military line. They were in the main law-abiding citizens, clergymen, pensioners and ardent young students, not militant agitators with Molotov cocktails. Windswept, their clothes sodden, their morale seeped away, was this as far as their protest could go? To shout out their abhorrence of the nuclear plant to have their words lost unheard to the bitter wind?

They had begun the long march as strangers, during the journey, natural leaders among them had led decision making. This group huddled together, heads down against the relentless driving wind to work out what to do.

To add to their discomfort, some of the protestors had seen weird movement in a field close to Brathay. They dismissed this as some locals, probably just kids having a bit of mischievous fun at the offcomer marchers' expense. As the protesters milled about, shivering with the cold, exhausted and demoralised, people at the back of the march yelled out in surprise. A few fell over, others turned and fled back towards Eskscale as a wave of underground turbulence rippled beneath their feet. Panicking and unable to move forward, the marchers joined their escaping comrades by bolting back to the village and beyond.

The earth's silent disturbance rippled long enough to clear the approach to Brathay. With the ground beneath the soldiers guarding the plant not targeted, they watched, bemused and puzzled as the well organised protesters became a disorganised fleeing rabble. A few of the younger soldiers broke into uneasy laughter at the marchers' sudden disarray and panic. One stern glance from a sergeant instantly stifled their mirth. What the hell was going on?

Spotting the curious stillness of the ground in Ryecroft field, four of the younger, fitter marchers headed for that, seeking safer ground. Unseen by anyone with the soldiers' focus on the break-up of the protest march, they never made it to the far side of the field. Their bodies dragged deep beneath the earth as blood tribute to a monstrous angry entity lurking there.

13

'They've gone … all of them away from the heft.'

Jed Barrows had burst into the farm house leaving his hard pushed tractor outside the farmhouse door, engine still running and alarming his family with his shocked expression. Flora stood up sharply, a mug of hot tea falling unnoticed onto the kitchen table. What could have distressed her normally unruffled man so badly? His Herdwick flock would never leave their area of the Fells, they were linked to it by ten thousand years of inherited instinct, they were hefted sheep that needed no walls or fences to keep them on their land.

'All of the flock have gone,' he continued, running a hand through his thick, greying dark hair, 'not a tup or yow left behind.'

As if in answer, the family dogs began to growl and whine, their hackles raised, the cats, their tails fluffy with alarm, shot out of the kitchen's open door. Outside in the yard, the three Fell ponies were kicking at their stable doors with frantic determination. Something bad was frightening the livestock, driving them to flee the safety and familiarity of the farm.

'Everyone, we must take heed of the warning from our beasts,' Flora declared, reaching for her coat, 'Ash, make sure your sheep in the home paddock are able to flee. Rowan, no arguing, let the ponies out, let them flee up the Fells too. Open up the coop doors for the hens and geese.'

She turned to Jed.

'Darling, get the Land Rover ready, I will grab coats and some food.'

No one argued with Flora, the sense of serious wrongness had now affected the less sensitive humans, reached some deep, primitive sense of warning. The others rushed out to follow her orders. Something bad was going to happen; the animals knew but how would Eskscale's people react? As much as she wanted to follow the sheep to higher ground, she needed to go down to the village, to try to persuade people to get away. She also knew her husband would not allow her to go alone no matter how much she insisted he stayed with the children.

Her daughter was the first to return, trying but failing to wipe away her tears. Rowen's awareness of danger was strong, maybe as potent as her mothers. Watching their much-loved Fell ponies gallop away without hesitation was a chilling sight. What was it that terrified them so much to make them bolt from the safety and comfort of the farm?

'Rowan, my love. You drive well enough to take Ash and the dogs in my car up to Scafell Pike … no arguments, we will join you up there … animals and birds are heading for higher ground, so must we. I don't know what will happen or how much time we have, but we must go higher.'

Flora threw coats, blankets and food in the Austin's wide boot, then paused, believing her children would be distraught and protest as she continued to speak.

'But first, I must warn the villagers. I sense they will be in the greatest danger.'

She exchanged looks with her daughter, relieved to see a stead, calm glance in return.

A tearful Flora watched her children, family dogs and

a farm cat with a litter of new born kittens drive off in her tough old Austin, heading to the hamlet of Wasdale Head, at the foot of Scafell Pike, the nearest high point up the Fells. She sighed with relief as it sped out of view. This was not a time for Rowan to test her independence by heading anywhere else but she knew in her heart she could trust her daughter. Jed pulled up beside her in the Land Rover, revving the engine, eager to get the mission done and be away to follow the children to Scafell.

'There's that protest March to contend with too,' he muttered, his features tightened into grim determination, 'all those offcomers to persuade, somehow.'

'I'll find a way, I have to ...'

Flora's answer dwindled as the enormity of her task hit home. How could she convince complete strangers they were in mortal danger without her knowing why?

Anson trusted the woman. Once awake, she had introduced herself and when prompted, spoke at some length of her life.

'I am no wild-eyed fanatic, Mr Anson. Just an ordinary woman who lived through the Blitz in London. I saw my family home burn to the ground with my parents' bodies trapped beneath the blazing rubble. My fiancé just another dead soldier on a Normandy beach.'

She wiped away another tear from so many already shed. 'I hate war, but none more so than nuclear.'

She was clearly a nice and perfectly normal woman. Enough to take advantage of her presence and leave for a secret meeting in the back room of The Herdwick Tup Inn. It was the first time in many months he'd been able to get out at night, Gary was tucked up in bed safe, yet still a lingering feeling of guilt at leaving his son, even for a few hours haunted Anson's steps down into Eskscale.

The storm had passed but the trees still dripped from their last lingering leaves onto the rain-slicked road. Fresh fallen leaves from the gale made the going slippery and treacherous. Anson decided not to drink to excess or risk a fall on the way home. Who would look after Gary if he injured himself further? Without work, he relied on the charity of the nuclear plant to give him a small pension and the cottage rent free after the accident.

Movement ahead of him paused his journey, the sickening fear of recognition spread, paralysing him. It was as if a piece of the darkness had taken form and approached him with malign intent. The living shadow was not alone, another formed from the night to be joined by three more. If it wasn't for the dim, ambient light from stars, they would have been close to invisible, save for the fierce glow from their red eyes.

Whimpering with fear, Anson backed into the hedge, seeking shelter from the horrors within the dense, prickling hawthorn and hazel. Silently, the Drood Men stalked the lane, seeking prey. One spotted the crouching man and darted toward him, splayed wide taloned fingers stretched before it. Even without the creature touching his face, he could feel an icy stroking of his radiation burns triggering a pain that went deep beneath his skin, tissue and muscle and into his skull.

Within feet of the quaking Anson, they paused, puzzled as a loud rumbling noise approached. Headlights from an oncoming car caught them, frozen into indecision. Anson saw for the first time that their faces had no mouth, no nose or ears, just those glaring red eyes. Their slick, black bodies snaked and twisted as if boneless, their extra-long taloned fingers went to protect their eyes against the headlight glare, exposing a veined, thinly stretched membrane like a bat's wing.

Then they were gone. Dissolving into the night leaving a lingering memory of their unearthly malice tangible in Anson' mind like a stain. Every instinct screamed to get back to the cottage, to his son. He knew he needed to attend the meeting of locals who knew about the Drood Men, who he prayed might know how to send them back into the Stones but his son was in danger. That was all that mattered now.

He ran back up the road, panic speeding every step. The car that saved him from the monsters, pulled up beside him. A young man in a suit, a boffin from Brathay working late, opened the passenger door wide for Anson.

'I am not going crazy, am I?'

Pale faced, the man stuttered, attempting to light up a cigarette with his hands shaking as Anson took his seat.

'No son,' Anson sighed, holding the man's hand steady to help him light up, 'I wish you were. I wish we both were. Please, hurry … I need to get back home to my son before those things reach him.'

Gary was not tucked up in bed, but sitting on the parlour couch, sipping a mug of steaming hot chocolate with Miss Brown: she was far too grown up to be called Yolanda as she had insisted. Was it a dream? A nightmare sound waking him … or reality? Something scratching at his bedroom window had sent Gary running, screaming down the stairs into the waiting arms of the babysitter.

'Just some twigs scraping at your window in those

high winds,' she had soothed as she mixed a generous measure of cocoa powder with sweetened hot milk. Gary had not replied. There were no trees or shrubs close to the house. She went upstairs to fetch his dressing gown, unable to resist peeking out of the window to reassure herself it was just a child's bad dream or over active imagination. His unease was shared. The terrier would not settle but paced the floor from front to back door, over and over again, whining and giving little throaty growls.

This did not help Yolanda's attempt to make light of the boy's fear. She felt it too. A creeping sensation of being watched by many unearthly eyes. Ridiculous! Chastening herself for such nonsense, she left the boy and the worrity little dog, strode up the stairs and into the boy's bedroom to look out of the only small window.

At first there was just darkness but as her eyes became adjusted to the star-lit gloom, she caught darting movement in the small garden in front of the house. Stifling a scream, Yolanda counted five impossible black figures, snake-like yet almost human. Her hand went to her mouth and bit down hard in an attempt to keep control of her panic, remembering the sinister shadow figure she'd seen at the Stones. One halted and turned its head up at the bedroom window. Its eyes like oval flames lit up an otherwise featureless face, one to her horror fixed directly on her.

She pulled back from the window but not before more red glowing eyes peered into the window from the side. These horrors could fly! Yolanda shrieked, pulled the curtains tight across and fled down the stairs. She ran from front door to back, pulling tight the bolts before fetching a kitchen knife and grabbing Gary from the sofa.

'They are here, aren't they?' he murmured, eyes huge with fear, 'The Drood Men.'

Unable to lie, the woman nodded, holding Gary in a tight, protective embrace, brandishing the knife in front of her. The scratching and scrabbling at the windows grew in ferocity, beyond that the only sound was the crisp rustle of their wing membranes.

'Why are they here?' Gary whispered, his body quaking in her arms.

Yolanda Brown did not answer, could not answer. Every certainty, every comfort from her world had been shattered by cruel, inhuman talons and the flurry of dark wings.

Flora and Jed had never seen so many vehicles parked haphazardly outside the Herdwick Tup. The hot oil reek of their hard driven engines hung in the air. As they climbed down from their equally hard pushed Land Rover, they both gave an involuntary shudder. The atmosphere was laden with a curious silence and overwhelming sense of deep dread. It was as if the land and its creatures had stopped, frozen in time, aware of an oncoming disaster, the like of which had never been known in this ancient, rugged land. The ambiance was not improved once inside the tavern which was murky with cigarette and pipe fug and the smell of fear triggered sweat. The arrival of Jed and Flora Barrows triggered a ripple of audible relief. Jed for his old Eskscale family history and no nonsense, down to earth attitude, and his wife for her knowledge of the old ways, the deep, primal earth magic from before missionaries from a middle eastern messianic sect came to these shores. If anyone knew what was going on and how to stop it, that would be Flora. With a sinking heart, once again she saw their faces turning to her with expectation. She took in a deep breath, pausing to compose herself as she prepared to crush their hope with the news that she had no idea what was happening nor how to stop it.

The Tup's landlady, Maggie Graham, approached the Barrows, with two large brandies. She had already gathered from the couple's expression that they were not bringing good news.

'Have a good long swig on the house,' she said handing them the glasses, 'I tek it your beasts have fled t' hills too.'

Jed gave a curt nod, glancing across the crowded pub, noting many Fell farmers among the villagers. A disappointing number of the offcomers, maybe they were too new to the area to be affected by the aura of wrongness. There were no strangers from the day's protest march, were they too afraid of angry locals to risk pausing at the pub. As if reading his thoughts, Maggie continued,

'Nobbut left of them protesters, appen they had enough of our wet, cold weather. Train were packed t' gills with them earlier, they all looked well flaiten too.'

A voice at the back of the bar spoke up, the vicar Rev Winters,

'Maybe we all should, get all the families together including the offcomers and on the next train away from here.'

'And tell them what, Rev?' yelled a voice from the other side of the bar, 'We know nothing beyond our livestock fleeing our farms.'

Jed raised his hand to quieten the rumble of voices.

'All the beasts are heading for high ground; I suggest we do the same … right now.'

Flora felt their attention return to her, feel their expectation as a tangible as the sturdy chair back she clung onto for support. So much hope and so much disappointment to come.

'My husband is right, we can all sense something bad is going to happen. There has never been a time when all the sheep on the Fells have left their heft at the same time. Our ponies bolted away too.'

'So you cannot stop it?'

Demanded a querulous, familiar voice, Ed Thwaite, already sacked from Brathay for shirking and petty pilfering.

'I need to know what is happening first, Mr Thwaite.

The boffin's car span into tyre-burning halt in front of the Anson's cottage. A home under siege. Horrified, Anson threw all safety to the wind, his son was in danger from the monsters. From the Drood Men feared by Eskscale's villagers for countless centuries but kept at bay by burying the Stones beneath tons of soil. He ran from the car, waving his arms, bellowing like a madman. Startled, the creatures shrank back, long enough for Anson to pound on the locked door and slip through a narrow gap.

The driver remained in the car, revving the engine hard and keeping the headlights at full beam. It seemed to alarm the creatures but for how long? He was no coward and though he wanted to release the car into a headlong flight down to the village he refused to give into his fear while a family was in danger.

An upstairs window opened, Anson appeared and managed to bellow a command before a monster flew up to the window. The man shut it just in time leaving the fright scratching at the glass in impotent fury. Jones had his orders, releasing the handbrake, he floored the accelerator with a stamp of relief and drove the short distance to Eskscale and The Herdwick Tup.

Slamming the Morris into a screeching halt outside the pub, Rhys Jones hurtled in through the door, oblivious to his wild-eyed and near hysterical appearance. He ranted, near to collapse, about Anson and his son being in danger from winged monsters, expecting to be ejected from the pub as a lunatic or arrested for a breach of the peace.

Instead, a group of older men and women took him to a quiet room at the back of the pub and someone conjured up a large measure of neat brandy, which Jones downed in one gulp. A handsome woman with long, titian red hair worn in a braid and wise, calming amber eyes, took his hands.

'You have nothing to fear from us, young man. We are people who have lived under the threat of what some call the Drood Men, for many years. We believe every word you have said. The shadows have become corporate beings and have left the cursed field. I believe they are very dangerous now.'

Jones looked up into her kind eyes and pleaded, 'Then for love of God, there is no time to talk. We must go and save the Ansons from these monsters.'

'We don't know how.'

Looking up at another speaker, a sturdy, handsome man, a farmer perhaps, Jones could see the fear in his eyes. Glancing at the circle of locals, they all shared that terror. There was no solution, no master plan. Just a pub full of frightened villagers unwilling to face the terrors waiting for them in the night.

'But I trust my wife to do all she can.'

The farmer put his hands on the red-haired woman's shoulders, gave them a comforting squeeze. Yet no one moved from their seats. Angry, Jones found the strength to stand and brush past these would be saviours.

'I'm not leaving those people to those things. I am going back.'

He went to the door, paused. 'If any of you have any damn backbone, bring torches, anything that has a bright light. That seems to disturb them.'

Jones rose from his seat and stormed out of the pub. As he got back into his car, the woman arrived at the car door and sat on the passenger seat. Her husband joined them in the back seat. She held out her hand to Jones.

'Flora Barrows, local folklorist, keeper of the old secrets and village witch and this is my husband, Jed, a farmer from another old Eskscale family.'

She smiled at the expected raised eyebrow over her mention of witch.

'My dear boy, we would never leave you alone to face those things, we are not the monsters in Eskscale.'

Jones heard many other vehicles revving behind him and wiped away tears of relief.

'This little community has lived with this secret for untold centuries. Now we must confront it,' Flora murmured, her voice betraying her rising fear. 'Something terrible has been awakened. I believe the power plant is the cause.'

Jones answered with a new conviction.

'I don't believe, Mrs Barrows. I know it is.'

'What do they want with us?'

Yolanda Brown still held onto the boy, her fiercely protective instincts only just overcoming the rising hysteria within. The number of creatures outside the door appeared to have increased, their clamouring wing beats and incessant scratching at windows and doors louder and persistent. Though they made no other sound, a tangible wave of their anger and malice seeped into the cottage, contaminating every room with threat.

Anson shook his head, now armed with everything he could find, kitchen and fishing knives, a garden hoe while the woman gripped a carving knife. Even young Gary had armed himself with a Swiss army knife and a heavy solid clothes iron. They knew they looked ridiculous but those things would not win without a fight.

'I wish I knew,' Anson replied, 'there once was an occasional rare sighting of a Drood Man, but mostly just lies and boasting from village lads trying to impress. Nothing like this.'

'Something has upset them, Da,' whispered the boy, 'upset them enough to fully rise from the Stones as something more than just shadows.'

That made sense. And Anson believed he knew what it was. If these monsters from ancient legend could exist, then so could the thing they were said to guard deep beneath the earth. Something disturbed by the nuclear plant? It had to be that, what else had changed in the area? But that did not explain their fixation on him and his home. Or did it? One maimed hand went up to his face, Anson had been poisoned by the plant. His skin was still radioactive, though according to all the experts, at a miniscule, harmless level. Anson knew they were lying, he could tell by their expressions, the way they could not make eye contact with him. What if the Drood Men could detect the toxic waste at any amount? He was a living part of what angered their master.

'Damn and blast'

Jones halted his car close to the Ansons' cottage, with the convoy of volunteers braking behind him. Immediately some of the Drood broke away and began to attack the cars, scratching at the windows and lashing the vehicles with their barbed tails. Clearly their fear of bright lights was short-lived, now they were unbothered by the headlights and torches, even when shone directly into their blazing ember eyes.

Strong taloned fingers wrenched open doors and hauled the screaming occupants out, throwing them onto the road. They stood in a circle around the trembling, bruised humans, their intent unknown, the only movement the flicker of their fire eyes and menacing swish of their long, barbed tails.

After what seemed a lifetime, one stepped forward and approached their captives. With no mouth it projected directly into their minds, assaulting them with a cacophony of loud discordant sound so piercing it burst eardrums and made ears bleed. The humans attempted to shut it out, their hands clamped tightly to their ears in a futile attempt to block the noise before it quietened to settle into a pattern resembling an actual language. One no one could speak. Familiarity shuddered through the Welsh scientist, no longer faint, the same voices that haunted his nightmares, now spoke with a new clarity.

This inability to communicate further enraged the Drood, showing their agitation with fluttering wings. Their frustration grew to dangerous levels, the air heavy with menace. Rhys Jones raised his arms and bravely stepped closer to the Drood 'spokesman.'

'It sounds close to Welsh, very old Welsh,' he shouted back to the villagers, 'It's a long shot, but I may be able to communicate with them. Unless any of you can still speak Cumbric?'

Nobody replied. He wasn't expecting an answer, the Brythonic language of the area had been extinct for centuries. Pushing aside the attempts at restraining him, Jones strode forward towards the nearest creature. Every instinct screamed at him to run for his life, but in a surge of inner steel, he stood his ground. The Drood insinuated its serpentine form to pause in front of him, its whiplash tail snaked around the Welshman's neck but did not tighten. Again, sound filled Jones' mind, formless at first, then the strange archaic language settled into a more familiar form of his native tongue.

Jones heard gasps from the watching crowd as someone forced his way through their throng. A wild-eyed man, impossible to age due to his extreme disarray, long hair filthy and matted, clad in torn, dirty and malodorous clothes. The gasps turned to screams as he pulled out a tarnished silver sickle from his inner coat pocket. He cleared the way through, brandishing it with the clear intent he would cut down anyone who clocked his passage to the front of the crowd.

The young Welshman heard Flora Barrows scornfully mutter a name, 'Bernard Stanley. So he must be the murdering bastard that has plagued Eskscale. I knew it had to be human, a madman.'

The name was vaguely familiar, something about a teacher who worked on uncovering the Stones? One of the Drood slunk towards Stanley, grabbing him by the throat, hauling him over to the others. Understandably the man was terrified, his face an ashen study in shock and disbelief, keening in wordless fear. The sickle fell from his hand and landed on the ground in front of the Drood.

'I did all you commanded,' he managed to mutter, bitter with indignation, 'I have been a loyal servant to your Master. I deserve to be rewarded for my loyalty.'

Once more, Jones heard the Drood's eerie voice in his mind.

'Our master, the Great Sea God, Nuada slumbers beneath this place. He is not to be disturbed, for his displeasure will rend this world to shattered cinders floating through an indifferent void. The universe will not know of this planet or its people and never will. All will be dust, dispersed by solar winds into total oblivion.'

Disturbed? By the building of Brathay power plant? No sooner had he thought those words, the creature responded with fury, tightening its tail. It was painful but Jones could still breathe. Just. Had he touched a raw nerve in the monster? Was his theory correct?

'Stop! Let me speak.'

Their other human captive managed to shuffle forward, eyes wide, shining with his madness.

'I have to talk for the sleeping god's guardians. You must understand. It's the poison! The radioactive poison that seeps into the earth and straight into the sea. That must stop now or the God will rise from His rest and destroy this world as a worthless orb of rock and water contaminated by us, to Him we are mere primates. We are as nothing in the great cosmic scheme.'

Radioactive waste? It had to be, agreed Jones through his own desperation and fear, his theory proven that it was Brathay's casual, careless disposal of the unnatural effluent of splitting the atom. The monster holding him continued,

'*We were charged with protecting the Great God's healing peace. We will stop the poison draining into the earth, flowing into the water, dispersing into the air. If you try to stop us, we will awaken the God and let him crush this planet to dust.*'

Without waiting for a reply, it released Jones who collapsed to the ground, holding his bruised neck and gasping for air.

'*Let us try to close it down first,*' he managed to shout at the creature's retreating form. '*We have evidence now ... a man injured by water from Brathay.*'

The Drood paused and sent words into Jones' mind again.

'*The dying, poisoned one has already been examined. The toxin cannot be contained. We will act tonight in ending this threat to our master.*'

'*Tonight? But we need more time to shut down the plant*'

The Drood's voice echoed with their collective contempt.

'*You have been warned, so many times and nothing was done. Enough! A great rising of the earth, then a flood, one so huge the sea will devour the land and bury the evil wrought by the infesting human creatures beneath a mountain of sand, rock and earth.*'

'Let me go ...'

Panicking, Stanley interrupted in a loud, shrill voice. He had risen to his knees, his hands clasped together, pleading,

'My family have always held the sacred promise, we have kept the Stones safe and unmoved since early times. I obeyed your command to have restored them to their former glory above the ground. Sacrificed to your kind with human blood as decreed in the ancient covenant. I have given Him many sacrifices, a holy woman and a virgin youth! Many strong, healthy men. I have not betrayed Nuada. My only plea is for freedom and a chance to escape His wrath.'

Irritated by Stanley's noise in a language it did not understand, the nearest Drood snapped the man's neck with a strong taloned hand. It ripped off Stanley's head and threw it into the appalled crowd of humans, spattering them with steaming blood. Even in the midst of this insanity Flora's heart twisted with anger and grief, now convinced that the bastard had murdered Freddie, the virgin youth of Stanley's declaration. With the man slain, she knew she would never know for sure.

His legs weak, a deeply shocked Jones glanced back to the waiting crowd from Eskscale, traumatised by the sight of these creatures and their callous ease when killing the wretch who had served them. So many faces locked in fearful rigor, maybe too shocked to take in what was happening. Jones turned back to address the Drood leader in Welsh, not wishing to suffer Stanley's horrible fate by babbling in a language they had no understanding of.

'There have been no warnings! Give us a chance to stop the contamination.'

One by one, the Drood faded back into the darkness, leaving one behind.

'Our task begins tonight, by dawn there will be nothing here but the sea.'

Returning to a more smoke like form, the Drood merged into the night leaving behind near silence, broken by fearful sobs. Jones relayed the creature's doom-laden message to the terrified gathering which had now been joined by Anson with his young son in his arms and an offcomer older woman.

'There is no time to debate,' Flora announced, 'we

must evacuate the village immediately, make a run for higher ground.'

'Impossible,'

'How much time do we have?'

'Can they be stopped?'

The desperate questions from the gathering stopped. A low, deep rumble beneath their feet grew in intensity, a burgeoning earthquake with no natural origin. Flora Barrows raised her hand to quell the panic, very much becoming the strong, tribal, wise woman of ancient times.

'Ring out the church bells, crank up the old air raid sirens, fire alarms,' she commanded, 'anything to get people out of their homes and into as many vehicles we can muster. We may not be able to save everyone but we must try.'

Rhys Jones knew a better way. He threw his car keys to Anson. 'Get your boy away from here. There is one way to get every living soul running from Eskscale and the farms around here. The emergency alarm at Brathay.'

Anson grabbed his arm, tried to stop him.

'I'll do it. I am no fool, I know these burns will kill me one day. You are a young man with your whole life ahead of you.'

'Then I suggest you use what time you have left to be with your son.'

Jones pushed the older man away hard, with enough force to send him sprawling onto the floor among the others. Worsening, the ground beneath them quivered, seeming more liquid than solid earth. Using the distraction, Jones bolted back towards Brathay, using willpower alone to keep his footing on the rippling ground. To his relief, no one followed and he could hear the rumble of many cars speeding away from the village.

It was a small comfort the nuclear plant was not close to a large city; the death toll would have been catastrophic.

With the protesters long dispersed, he had no trouble getting past the wire barrier, now with a section pulled back to let the technicians and scientists access to their workplace. His lungs burned, close to collapse as he fell through the main entrance to the plant. In desperation, Jones managed to pull himself together, trying to walk calmly through the compound. He could not risk screaming at the waiting security guards and their military backup to flee for their lives from Brathay. They would have detained him as a dangerous lunatic. Better they remembered he was a top boffin, no doubt eccentric, who had left something behind in his office.

He needed not have worried, the security men and the soldiers at the plant hardly noticed the young Welshman passing through the gates. The deepening earthquake was spreading fear, many had decided the plant was in danger of exploding and had bolted from their posts. Inside, Jones spotted his close colleagues, desperately seeking a cause, running from the control rooms in confusion. The panels did not lie, whatever was causing the restless earth, it wasn't the nuclear plant. He ran to his friends.

'Craig! Jean! Get the rest of the team out of here, for God's sake, save your lives.'

Without waiting to make sure his colleagues had fled, Jones found the main alarm and set off the deafening banshee screech that would resound far across the landscape.

An armada of over-crowded cars, tractors, lorries and buses rode out as the heaving land, bucked beneath their

RAVEN DANE

wheels like a furious wild horse. In the headlong flight, many lost tyres, broke axles, ran out of fuel but were towed by the others vehicles. Not all the locals had fled. Many remained, from fear, disbelief, or unwillingness to leave their property. Farmers had already found their livestock had made their own choice, bolting for higher ground from deep ingrained instinct long before the first rumble of the unstable earth.

Anson had crammed the Morris with as many as he could. A couple and their three young children in the back, Yolanda in the front passenger seat, holding his dozing son. He halted the Welsh scientist's car at a viewing point along the high ridge of Scafell Pike, the first foothills of the mountainous Lake District which were mercifully within close reach. Already the night had given way to the pale grey light of early dawn. The roar of the quaking earth that had deafened them on their escape had ceased and like a deep intake of breath, an uneasy silence fell across the land below. Anson prayed the heroic young man had found a way to escape the Droods' terrible threat, there were still many vehicles passing, fleeing to higher ground. There was still hope for him.

He shuddered as a dark line grew along the sea horizon, moving inland at astonishing speed and growing in height with every second. Anson reached over gave his son a tight hug then restarted the overcrowded Morris, not daring to look behind as the tidal wave swept in to overwhelm the land. He would not stop until the hoped for safety of the high Lakeland Fells.

Behind and below him, the monstrous wave crashed down upon the land with a force more powerful than all the nuclear bombs made by Mankind. Within seconds,

146

Brathay, the Stones and Eskscale were gone, submerged by the fury of an ancient deity. But what of the others? There were other nuclear plants planned for many coastal towns of Great Britain. Would Nuada's rage spread to these? To power plants around the whole world?

Anson shivered, his blood icy with fright but he could not give in to despair, not with his son slumbering in Yolanda's arms, counting on him to keep him safe, make things right. Without a backward glance, he drove on into an uncertain future.

Kneeling on the ground, unaware someone had thrown a wool car blanket across his shoulders, Rhys Jones' haggard features had aged his appearance by several decades. His eyes were red-rimmed, deep troughs ran from his eyes down his cheeks from his unchecked weeping. Though his skin and clothes were bone dry, his body shivered. He had not spoken nor had any coherent thoughts but Jones' mind replayed images on a continuous reel. The blazing eyes of the Drood Men, the banshee scream of the power plant's alarm, the race for life against the tumultuous wall of seawater. He dimly remembered a Land Rover pulling up beside him as he ran from Brathay, of being hauled into the vehicle by strong arms. Jed Barrows' arms.

And worse of all, as he and the farmer's family reached the high ground, the sickening debris of ruined lives crashing against the side of the fell. Homes reduced to splintered wood and shattered brick, mighty trees cut down like straw, battered to nothing but pulped remains. The swirling debris mixing with animal and human victims, now unidentifiable flesh and bone shards. Were people he knew part of that carnage? Were Jean and Craig, his good friends among the dead?

His mind rang with a sound too, deeper and below the booming roar of the tidal wave, a vengeful bellow of unearthly yet sentient triumph. A woman's gentle voice interrupted the memory of that terrifying sound.

'Maybe we are the guilty ones.'

Exhausted and shivering with shock, Flora sank to the sodden ground besides the young scientist. Wiping away her own tears, she continued.

'The old Eskscale families always knew terrible danger lurked beneath our soil but they kept it secret.'

'Why wouldn't they?' Jones replied with an anger rising from deep within his soul, 'who would have believed them? Uncovering those Stones was inevitable as modern science progressed. It was us, the offcomers with our arrogance and callous neglect that poisoned the earth and water with radiation. I tried to warn them, tried to stop them ...'

His voice trailed off as he collapsed sobbing, as the enormity of the destruction and loss of life came crashing down on his conscience. Ashen-faced, Jed and the younger ones arrived to join them, accompanied by the family's quivering, fearful dogs. All the world the Barrows family had known, all that they possessed had been destroyed.

No one spoke, what more was there to say?

Epilogue

Nuada, was once known as the Sea God of the ancient Britons. An entity who had fought and slain so many powerful celestial enemies, was now wounded and in grievous need of rest. His shadow creatures had rounded up the sentient beings of Earth and put them to work. A thousand years of their labour had built him a sanctuary deep beneath the soil and rock. His enemies would not seek him there, expecting him to hide beneath the deep ocean of the little blue planet. The last generation of humans to toil for the god had been released, unharmed, for they passed down their memories and fireside tales to keep this place sacrosanct, undisturbed. One strong bloodline of these primates was given great rewards for protecting the site. With the unearthly creatures' task completed, they became spirits and rested beneath the Stones.

Until the poison came, seeping through the earth and water, tainting the god's resting place. This would not be tolerated. Not on that land on the edge of the sea, not anywhere on that miserable, primate infested planet.

About The Author

Raven Dane is a UK based author of dark fantasy, alternative history, steampunk novels and horror short stories. Her first books were the dark fantasy *Legacy of the Dark Kind* trilogy. These were followed by a High Fantasy spoof, *The Unwise Woman of Fuggis Mire*. Her steampunk novels are the award-winning *Cyrus Darian and the Technomicron* and *Cyrus Darian and the Ghastly Horde*. She has had many short stories published, including one in a celebration of forty years of the British Fantasy Society and in many international horror anthologies. These have included Crystal Lake's *Tales of the Lake* 2 and *Shallow Waters* Volume 2. She also had a story in *Frightmare – Women Write Horror* which was shortlisted for a prestigious Bram Stoker award in 2016. She also has short stories in anthologies in the Gruesome Grotesque series published by TK Publishing and in a range of anthologies edited by Dean M Drinkel.

In 2013, she was signed up by Telos Publishing for her collection of Victorian ghost stories, *Absinthe and Arsenic* and in 2015, the alternative history/ supernatural novel, *Death's Dark Wings*. All the Cyrus Darian books are now with Telos. The third book in the series, *Cyrus Darian and the Wicked Wraith* was launched in August 2019 by Telos.

A lifelong *Doctor Who* fan, Raven was delighted to be part of the script team on a spin off film, *The White Witch of Devil's End* by Reeltime Pictures in 2017. She also contributed to the novelisation of the film, published by

Telos.

Raven brought out a horror novella, *The Bane of Bailgate* in 2018.

Her novella set in a chaotic, dystopian future, *The House of Wrax* was launched by Demain Publishing in 2020 to enthusiastic reviews from Science Fiction critics.

Also with Demain Publishing, Raven was honoured to be chosen to have a short story in an anthology based in the grim world of the Quiet Apocalypse novellas by celebrated author Dave Jeffreys.

Her scurrilous parody of High Fantasy, *The Unwise Woman of Fuggis Mire* was republished in 2022 with a beautiful new cover.

Raven is currently working on a dark fantasy novel titled *Esoterique*.

Also by Raven Dane

NOVELS

DEATH'S DARK WINGS

CYRUS DARIAN SERIES
1: CYRUS DARIAN AND THE TECHNOMICRON
2: CYRUS DARIAN AND THE GHASTLY HORDE
3: CYRUS DARIAN AND THE WICKED WRAITH

SHORT STORY COLLECTIONS

ABSINTHE & ARSENIC